CATCH A
FALLING STAR

Books by Beverly Lewis

SUMMERHILL SECRETS

Whispers Down the Lane
Secret in the Willows
Catch a Falling Star
Night of the Fireflies

THE HOLLY'S HEART SERIES

Holly's First Love
Secret Summer Dreams
Sealed With A Kiss
The Trouble With Weddings
California Christmas
Second-Best Friend
Good-bye, Dressel Hills
Straight-A Teacher
The "No-Guys" Pact
Little White Lies

THE CUL-DE-SAC KIDS

Double Dabble Surprise
Chicken Pox Panic
Crazy Christmas Angel
No Grown-ups Allowed
Frog Power
Mystery of Case D. Luc

CATCH A FALLING STAR

Beverly Lewis

BETHANY HOUSE PUBLISHERS
MINNEAPOLIS, MINNESOTA 55438

Cover illustration by Chris Ellison

Copyright © 1995
Beverly Lewis

Published by Bethany House Publishers
A Ministry of Bethany Fellowship, Inc.
11300 Hampshire Avenue South
Minneapolis, Minnesota 55438

Printed in the United States of America.

Library of Congress Cataloging-in-Publication Data

Lewis, Beverly
    Catch a falling star / Beverly Lewis.
        p.   cm. — (SummerHill secrets ; bk. 3)
    Summary: While working on a geneology project at the end of
eighth grade, Merry learns about her own family's Amish connection
and must decide how to handle the attention of Levi Zook, her Amish
neighbors' sixteen-year-old son.

    [1. Amish—Fiction. 2. Christian life—Fiction.] I. Title.
II. Series: Lewis, Beverly, 1949–   SummerHill secrets ; 3.
PZ7.L58464Cat   1995
[Fic]—dc20   95–30278
ISBN 1–55661–478–0   CIP
                                                            AC

To Dave,
with thanks for the simple gifts—
long walks and quiet talks . . .
and stargazing.

BEVERLY LEWIS is a speaker, teacher, and the best-selling author of the HOLLY'S HEART series. She has written more than twenty-four books for teens and children. Many of her articles and stories have appeared in the nation's top magazines.

Beverly is a member of The National League of American Pen Women, the Society of Children's Book Writers and Illustrators, and Colorado Christian Communicators. She and her husband, Dave, along with their three teenagers, live in Colorado. She fondly remembers their cockapoo named Cuddles, who used to snore to Mozart!

'Tis the gift to be simple.
'Tis the gift to be free.

—Old American Hymn

ONE

I probably would have ignored Lissa Vyner the rest of the school year and all summer, too, for doing what she did. In fact, I was one-hundred-percent-amen sure if Lissa hadn't been my friend I would have refused to have anything whatsoever to do with her.

Outrageous. That's what it was. How dare she ask Jonathan Klein to be her project partner! But she had. And I could still see her waiting outside social studies, all pert and confident with her wavy blond hair pulled back on one side, her blue eyes shining.

It wasn't as if Lissa was totally tuned out with no idea of how I felt. Months ago she'd even asked me point-blank if Jon was my boyfriend. Silly me, I'd changed the subject. The truth was, I truly admired Jon, maybe even the *L* word, but I'd tried desperately to keep all traces of such things hidden. Aside from the fact that he considered me his equal when it came to playing his alliteration game, I doubted Jonathan Klein even knew I existed—as a girlfriend, anyway.

"Who're you teaming up with?" I asked Chelsea Davis in the cafeteria line the next day.

She puffed out her cheeks and rolled her eyes as though

the assignment were something out of grade school. "You kidding? Why do we have to have partners to do a family history?"

"Well"—I wondered why she was so upset—"doesn't sound like such a bad idea to me. Might be kinda fun."

"I'd rather go bungee jumping over a pool of hungry sharks," she protested.

I reached for the soy sauce and sprinkled some on my chicken chow mein. "Maybe you'll uncover some never-before-discovered secrets. Don't *all* families have skeletons in their closets?" I rubbed my hands together.

She snickered.

"So . . . wanna be my partner?" I asked.

Chelsea gathered her super-thick auburn hair away from her face and flung it over her shoulder before picking up her tray. "I can see this is gonna be a kickin' good time."

"Truly?" I followed her to our table.

She laughed. "You're crazy, Merry Hanson."

"Good, then it's set." I dropped my schoolbag on the chair across from her. "We're a team."

Chelsea nodded nonchalantly.

Honestly, I was relieved. Last I checked, there were only a couple kids unclaimed as partners. One was Ashley Horton, our new pastor's daughter. Since Lissa had snatched up my number one choice, I was more than happy to settle for Chelsea. I don't mean that Ashley was all that bad. Actually, the girl had a lot going for her. Great smile, nice hair, and truly sweet—she wasn't a typical preacher's kid. In fact, she was the kind of girl most guys would easily fall for. Fall in love with, and then not be able to engage in decent conversation. At least that's how she struck me.

For that one reason I didn't want to link up with Ashley for the end-of-the-year project. Well, there was one other minuscule reason. Unfortunately, it had to do with Ashley making a not-so-subtle attempt last month at getting Jon's attention.

Sigh. Why did it seem as though every girl in Lancaster County was attracted to the Alliteration Wizard?

After lunch, I was opening my locker when I heard the familiar greeting. "Mistress Merry." I turned to see Jon hurrying down the hall toward me.

"Soon school'll be squat," he said, starting up our alliteration game as he stood beside my locker.

"Three more weeks and eighth grade's history." I looked up just in time to catch his heart-stopping smile.

"Say that with all *g*'s," he teased.

I could see Ashley at the end of the hall, fussing around in her locker. She primped in her mirror as though she didn't know what to do with herself. But I knew she was spying. Several lockers away from Ashley's, Lissa peered over her shoulder, glaring in my direction, no doubt longing to know what Jon and I were talking about.

Not wanting to clue in either girl as to Jon's and my word-game connection—after all, it was all we really had, and it was precious to me—I turned away from their surveillance and lowered my voice. I couldn't pass up an opportunity to show Jon my amazing intellectual stuff. "All *g*'s, you say?"

He nodded, enticing me. "Oh, you know, give or take a few."

"Goodbye grand and glorious grade of eight. Gimme ghastly halls of high school," I said.

He grinned at me—really grinned. Then he reached up and leaned on my locker door. "I take it you're not looking forward to freshman year?"

"Did I say that?" I shrugged, staring down at my tennies. His hand was touching my locker door! His arm was so close to me. So close . . .

I wondered if Lissa and Ashley were still gawking. Shrugging the thought away, I felt embarrassed admitting to my fellow classmate and word-game equal that the thought of high school sent me into jitterland.

"High school is just one step up from here, right?" he said. "No problem."

Maybe not for him.

I forced a smile. "I guess change is good."

He stepped back slightly and ran his free hand through his light brown hair. "Well, I guess it's all in how you look at it."

"Say that with all *y*'s," I said, eager for this conversation to last forever. But the hallway was cramming up with students, growing more noisy by the second. "Oh well, skip it."

"Later?" His brown eyes twinkled.

"Okay." But I had a feeling our wonderful word game was over, at least for today. And I was right.

By the end of the day, Lissa showed up at Jon's locker with a spiral notebook. Probably with talk of their social studies project. I was pretty sure she would monopolize him for the next three weeks. And after that, school would be out for the summer.

I hated the thought of summer vacation. For one thing,

I liked school, really and truly; it had nothing to do with seeing Jon every day. Fortunately, though, he attended the same church I did, and there were lots of youth services and special activities all summer long.

I peeked around my locker door the way Lissa and Ashley had done earlier. I made sure Lissa didn't catch me, though. As for Jon, it was impossible for him to spot my envious eyes—he was facing *her*.

Reaching for my math and social studies books, I was dying for one more glance. But it was a mistake—I never should've taken another look. Jon reached up and held on to her locker door exactly the way he had mine, while Lissa gazed up at him all dreamy-eyed.

Swiftly, I stuffed my books into my schoolbag and closed my locker. I needed some fresh air. Fast!

TWO

A bunch of kids were already waiting for the bus at the bottom of the steps of Mifflin Middle School—hallowed ground, in my opinion. With only a few days left as an eighth grader, I was entitled to feel this way about my school. Three solid years of memories—some good, some not. I consoled myself with the thought that I'd have all summer to get used to the idea of high school.

I turned around and scanned the steps, wondering when Lissa would show up. Usually, I sat with Chelsea on the bus, sometimes Lissa.

Today, I wanted to be alone. But I didn't plan to budge before I saw with my own eyes that Lissa's conversation with Jon was over.

The bus made the turn at the end of the drive, and the crowd of kids jammed up, moving toward the bold yellow lines. That's when I heard Jon's voice.

I turned to see him hold the door for Lissa, and she stepped out of the school like a princess. A golden glow graced her face, and I stared, trying to decide if the lustrous shine came from the sun illuminating her wheat-colored hair—or was it because of Jon's attentive smile?

A kid behind me yelled, "Keep it moving."

"Chill," I shot back and headed toward the bus.

Instead of sitting in the front as usual, I felt like going to the back of the bus and crawling under one of the seats. Especially now that it looked as though Jon and Lissa were going to keep talking. Through the smeared-up bus windows, I spotted them and felt my throat turn to cotton.

On my way to the rear of the bus, I passed Ashley Horton and several church friends sharing a bag of chips. Miss Preacher's Kid hardly noticed me. At least she didn't bother to say anything or glance my way.

Suddenly, I was hungry. Stress did that to me. Sliding into the last seat, I took refuge by leaning against the hard window. I watched Jon and Lissa as they stood side by side outside, still talking.

My stomach growled, and I reached into my schoolbag, pulled out an apple, and bit down hard. From my vantage point, I noticed Jon's hands gesturing rapidly as they often did when he talked. Lissa's eyes were incredibly bright. My guess was she was falling hard and fast. For *my* guy.

I chomped down on the next bite of apple, trying to compose myself. *Get it together, Merry. He's only being nice.*

"Whatcha doin' all the way back here?" Chelsea asked, plopping herself down next to me.

I forced my eyes away from the window. "Don't ask."

She glanced out the window. "Oh, *I* get it."

"Get what?"

"Not what, Mer—*who?*" And with that remark, she pointed toward the window.

I shoved her arm down. "Chelsea, please!"

"Oh, don't tell me . . ." She scrunched down, putting

her knees up against the seat in front of us. "This is one of those truly horrible days of your life, right?" She'd used my own words to mimic me!

It was bad enough being secretly in love with Jon, but having to observe him with someone else—especially a good friend—knowing they'd probably be going to each other's houses for the social studies project . . . well, it *was* truly horrible.

Then, to top things off, when the two of them finally did board the bus, Jon slid in next to Lissa—the seat where she and I usually sat. Not once did she check to see where I was sitting.

Friday afternoons weren't supposed to be like this. A girl ought to be able to go home from school feeling good for having done her best work all week long.

Do everything for the honor and glory of God, Mom always said. Dad, too, only he wasn't given to hammering away at his philosophies. For as long as I could remember, the concept had been drilled into my head. My brother's, too. And it must've worked for Skip because my brainy brother was going to graduate from high school with honors!

The bus jolted forward, and I tried my best not to look at Jon and Lissa even though they were smack dab in my line of vision. I took another slurpy bite of my apple and slumped down in my seat, pushing my knees up against the seat in front of me, copying Chelsea.

She smirked. "Now you're getting the hang of things. And just think, you won't have to ride this rotten bus again till Monday morning."

"Oh, terrific," I mumbled. But she was right. One good thing about today being Friday, I wouldn't have to suffer through another Lissa-and-Jon day till Monday. I could use a weekend about now.

Then I remembered. Sunday—church!

Surely Lissa wouldn't carry her newfound link with Jon through the weekend, drag it right into church, and parade it in front of me.

I must've gasped or something because Chelsea said, "What's wrong?"

"What?"

"Your face is all white, Mer."

"I'm fine, really." Then I changed the subject. "When do you want to start working on the family history assignment?"

"Never." Her sea green eyes looked sly.

"So, what about tomorrow?" I laughed.

"My house?" She pulled out her schoolbag and found her daily planner. "What time?"

"After lunch?" She wrote my name in the Saturday, May 13 box. "About one-thirty?"

Chelsea elbowed me. "Hey, maybe you'll get so absorbed in your past, you'll forget about your future." She jerked her head toward Jon.

"What a truly horrible thing to say!"

"Uh, there you go again," she teased. "Where do you get this, Mer? Truly this and truly that—c'mon!"

I sat up, mostly to create some distance between us. Then thumbing through my social studies book, I found the scribbled notes I'd made for the Hanson family tree project.

"Hey, don't take it seriously," Chelsea said, her voice softer now. "I was just kidding."

"Whatever." I shuffled the papers, frustrated with the world.

"Mind if I take a look?" she asked.

I relinquished my notes, not caring whether Chelsea read the details of my father's Swiss ancestors. Some of them had survived hideous treatment for their beliefs; other Anabaptists had been murdered.

Chelsea was suddenly quiet as she read through my pages of notes. "This is unreal," she said, referring to the martyrs, I guess. "How could they do it—I mean, just let someone torture them to death?"

"My dad says God gives people martyrs' grace."

"What's that?" She studied me with intense eyes.

"I think it means God softens the pain of dying somehow."

She scoffed. "Whoever heard of that!"

"Don't laugh," I said. "It's true."

"How would *you* know?"

I couldn't believe it. Just when I thought I was actually getting somewhere with her. In fact, every time I thought I was making spiritual headway with Chelsea, she'd pull something like this.

I refused to display my exasperation. "There are many examples recorded in the *Martyrs Mirror*."

"Martyrs what?"

"It's a German book a thousand pages long," I explained. "It's nearly sacred to the Amish. I've seen it lots of times at Rachel Zook's house."

"Your neighbors?"

I nodded. "Rachel says the book is really sad. It tells about men and women being murdered—their little children, even babies, being orphaned—all sorts of horrible things because of what they believed."

"Sounds awful."

She turned back to my notes, pouring over them as her thick, shoulder-length hair inched forward and dropped, hiding her face from view.

I stared out the window at lilac bushes in full bloom along SummerHill Lane. Leaning up, I opened the window and breathed in their sweet aroma. Then I settled down to finish off my apple.

Acres of meticulously plowed fields stretched away from the road for miles. Yards of neatly mown grass and elaborate flower beds with deep red and bright pink peonies were evident at one Amish farmhouse after another.

I began to relax as we rode toward the old house on the corner of SummerHill and Strawberry Lanes. There was something peaceful about this three-mile stretch. And after a day like today, I needed *something* soothing.

I glimpsed Rachel Zook, my Amish friend, and her younger sister Nancy working two mules in the field closest to the road. The mules were hitched to a cultivator, weeding the alfalfa—the preferred hay in Lancaster. I'd heard that in one growing season, it was possible for an Amish farmer to get as many as three or four cuttings—something to do with the land having a limestone base. I smiled as I watched Rachel handle the mules. She held the reigns loosely and, like the mules, could probably perform this job blindfolded.

I wondered how Rachel felt about completing her last year of school. She was almost fifteen, and the Amish only attended school through eighth grade. After that, girls helped with making and canning grape juice, "putting up" a variety of vegetables, bread-making, quilting, and keeping house. And waiting for marriage.

Rachel and a group of her Amish friends had started a "charity" garden on a one-acre plot on their land. They were in charge of planting and caring for the garden until harvest time, when they'd harvest the vegetables and freeze or can them. Later they would label the fruits of their labor and distribute the vegetables to several "English"—non-Amish—orphanages nearby. It was a garden of love.

Rachel and her mother would soon become a team in the female domain of getting garden produce from the soil to the kitchen table. And like most plain girls her age, Rachel was "running around" with a supper crowd on weekends and attending Sunday night singings where she could meet eligible young Amishmen.

On the north side of the house, Levi, Rachel's sixteen-going-on-seventeen-year-old brother, worked the potato field with his younger brother Aaron. Levi, tall and slender and the cutest Amish boy ever, was well into in his *Rumschpringa*—the Amish term for the running-around years. Amish parents loosened their grip on their teens long enough for them to experience the modern, English world. Most teens eventually returned to their Amish roots, got baptized, and settled down to marry and raise a family of seven or eight children.

Levi took off his straw hat and wiped his forehead on his arm. He must've spotted the school bus at that moment because he began to wave his hat. A wide, sweeping wave.

Surprised, I turned away. Amish boys weren't supposed to flirt with English girls. But Levi didn't seem to care about such things. He was *always* flirting with me—he'd even asked me to ride in his open courting buggy last month. He didn't know it, but I'd secretly nicknamed him Zap 'em Zook because of his wild and reckless buggy driving.

Living on adjacent properties had its advantages during our growing up years. All the Zook kids, except Curly John who was much older and married now, had been my playmates. In fact, once when all of us were swimming in the pond behind our houses, Levi got his foot stuck in a willow root under the water. None of the other kids seemed to notice he'd disappeared, but I had. Being a truly brave eight-year-old, I dove down and untangled his foot—seconds before his lungs would've given out.

I'd saved Levi's life. From that time on, he said he was going to "get hitched up" with me someday. Silly boy. Cute as he was, Levi Zook had beans for brains!

THREE

I wrapped my apple core in a tissue and stuffed it down into the corner of my schoolbag as the bus approached my house.

Chelsea straightened my social studies notes. "Here you go," she said, handing them to me. "I can't imagine letting someone set me on fire for believing in God. Too bad your ancestors didn't know they were dying for nothing."

She had that unyielding look on her face.

"God is real, Chelsea, whether you say so or not."

She gave me a half smile. "You're not gonna preach now, are you?"

It was her standard line. But I wasn't giving up on my self-proclaimed atheist friend. Not today, not ever!

"Well, here's my house. I'll see you tomorrow at one-thirty." I crawled over her to get to the aisle.

"See ya," Chelsea called.

I held on to the seat, waiting for the bus to stop. Even though I had to walk past Jon and Lissa, I didn't let their "Bye, Merry, have a great weekend" comments get to me.

Waiting for the bus doors to open, I realized something amazing. This social studies project was just what I needed to get my mind off less important things—present parties included! Talking about my ancestors had done the trick.

I hurried down out of the bus and ran up SummerHill to our sloping front lawn, around the side yard to the white gazebo, and collapsed on the steps.

My cats, Shadrach and his brother, Meshach, followed by my beautiful white kitten, Lily White, made their appearance from under the gazebo, looking plump and sleepy.

"Where's Abednego?" I inspected the dark, cool area beneath the gazebo.

My cats were not only beautiful, they were extremely intelligent. Their choice of a cool and carefree place to snooze was just one more indication of that.

I called for Abednego, who was always the last one to show up. Slowly, grandly, he emerged into the sunlight, squinting his eyes as he made his debut.

"Take your time, why don'tcha?" I teased him. But he wasn't moved by my words and came nuzzling up against my leg. "You think that's all it takes for an apology, huh?" I scooped him up and carried him to the house in my schoolbag.

Lily White scampered ahead of me, meowing for equal time. She and I didn't go back as far as the three Hebrew cat children, but Lily *was* extraspecial. Beautiful, and white as a lily. I had saved her life in Zooks' barn fire last month— risking mine to do it.

"Come on, little boys," I called over my shoulder. They did as they were told, obeying their mistress Merry to a tee. I choked down the thought of referring to myself that way— it only reminded me of my jovial Jon who was probably still sitting next to the light and lovely Lissa.

"Mom, I'm home!"

The kitchen smelled like rhubarb pie mingled with the aroma of roast beef. Clean and free of clutter, the kitchen sparkled as though the cleaning lady had just been here. But it was Friday, and Mrs. Gibson came on Tuesdays.

Something was up.

I dumped my schoolbag on a chair. Carefully, I lifted Abednego out of his hiding place and carried him to the counter. "Check this out," I said as we sniffed two big pies cooling near the window.

Mom came sailing through the room. "How was school, honey?" She kissed the air near my cheek, then scurried off to the dining room.

Lily White let out an irritated, whiny *meow*. Even though she loved *me*, she was still adjusting to the rest of the Hanson family.

"School? Oh, it was there." I couldn't tell Mom how school had really been. It involved talking about Jon, and no one needed to know that secret part of my life. "We're doing a cool assignment in social studies," I mentioned, opening the fridge.

"Oh?"

"Yeah, it's a good way to close out the school year." I poured some milk and crept into the spacious formal dining room to observe Mom—busy as usual.

"Why's that, honey?" She glanced up momentarily as though she was interested in a reply, but I could tell her mind was on other things. Like polishing silverware and wiping off her good china.

"Someone coming for dinner?" I asked.

She smiled, completely forgetting about my social studies project. "Some of your father's relatives are in town. They're staying at a bed and breakfast in Strasburg, but called to see if they could take us out to eat." She sighed, counting the salad forks. "I thought it would be just as well to invite them here. You know how your father likes to unwind after a long day at the hospital."

I smiled to myself. Mom sometimes liked to use Dad as an excuse to do things her way. Sure Dad would be tired from making rounds and treating patients, but it was really Mom who preferred to dine at home. Besides, this would be another opportunity for her to be the perfect hostess.

I wandered back into the kitchen, pouring fresh milk for the cat quartet. Eagerly, they crowded around the wide, flat dish, their pink tongues lapping up the raw milk straight from moo to you from the Zooks' dairy farm next door.

"Oh, Merry," Mom called from the dining room as though she'd forgotten something. "Someone else called—for you."

I hurried through the kitchen again. "Who? Someone from school?"

She straightened up, holding a fistful of spoons. "You know, it almost sounded like Levi Zook," she said, a curious look in her deep brown eyes. "There was background noise, though, like he was calling from town."

I frowned. "Didn't he say who he was?"

She shook her head. "I asked if he'd like to leave a message, but he seemed to be in a hurry."

"That's weird." I wondered what Levi was up to.

I asked for more details. "What kind of background noise did you hear?"

"Come to think of it, he may have been down at the Yod-

26

ers'—they have that new carpentry shop over in Leola." She carried the silverware into the kitchen.

I followed.

"But the Yoders are Amish, too," I reminded her. "They don't have a phone, do they?"

"Well, maybe they do," she said, searching for some silver polish under the sink. "More and more Amish are having phones installed in their businesses, but the way I understand it, they aren't allowed to use them for personal calls."

"So you really think it was Levi?"

"Almost positive."

"Hmm . . . okay, Mom. Thanks." Hurrying out of the kitchen, I headed down the long hall to the front staircase, carrying my book bag and a second glass of milk, this one spiked with a touch of chocolate syrup.

What does Levi want? I wondered.

Inside my room, I emptied my schoolbag, taking time to organize my books and notebooks on my desk—a massive white antique pine. Mom had found it at an estate auction years ago in disrepair. After stripping and repainting it white to match my corner bookcase, the old piece charmed my room like nothing else. Except for my wall gallery, of course, on the opposite side of the room.

I'd framed and displayed my best photography there, starting with pictures taken in first grade with my little camera. Cheap as the camera had been, the colors were still clear and bright.

Thoughts of Levi and Jon twirled in my head as I surveyed the entire wall. Recounting the pictures of my life was a kind of ritual. I drank in the tranquil scenes of Amish farmhouses, the willow grove, and a covered bridge not far from here. There were before-and-after pictures, too. Like the one of a fresh apple pie made by Miss Spindler, another neighbor, before and after it had been sliced into six pieces.

Last month I'd had a change of heart and decided to include pictures of people in my wall gallery. The decision was triggered by an incredible event that happened right after the Zooks' barn fire. Anyway, I now had enlargements of my favorite people displayed on the wall. People like Mom, Dad, and Skip posing in front of our ivy-strewn gazebo, Lissa and Chelsea hamming it up on the school bus.

But the best picture of all was one I'd taken as a little girl. It featured Faithie, my twin, before she got sick and went home to Jesus.

Mom had helped frame some of the pictures with bonafide antique frames, but she couldn't stand to have old relics around unless they were immaculate.

I wondered as I looked at Faithie's picture if my twin might have inherited Mom's interest in antique treasures had she lived past her seventh birthday. One thing was certain, Mom had not passed on her obsession with old things to me. It wasn't that I didn't appreciate them. I guess it had more to do with growing up with so many Amish neighbors—not to mention the ones way back in my family tree— and wanting to be my own person. A *very* modern girl.

I changed into white cutoffs and a red top, with red-and-white striped tennies to match. Then I headed into the bathroom adjoining my room and washed my face, careful not to smudge my mascara. A quick look in the mirror, and I grabbed a hairbrush. When my hair was smooth, I stepped back to scrutinize myself.

"Ready or not, here I come," I said out loud, eager to get over to the Amish farm next door.

It was time to set my friend Levi Zook straight. Once and for all.

FOUR

Mom was still busying herself with preparations for the evening meal when I darted through the kitchen. "Merry," she called just as I reached the screen door.

"Yes?" I turned around.

"Come tell me what you think," she said from the dining room. "I need your expert opinion."

In a hurry to see Levi, I rushed back through the kitchen and found my mom holding a matching set of white candle holders. "Which looks better?" She held them up dramatically, eyeing the floral centerpiece—pink and white roses scattered with babies' breath and greenery. "Do you like the table with or without the candles?"

I waited as she placed the candle holders on the table, one on either side of the white basket of flowers. "Without," I said. "Too formal with candles."

She stepped back, concentrating on the table. "Are you sure?"

"I'm sure, Mom. Why'd you ask me if—"

"Merry," she said, glancing at me. "You don't have to get upset about this."

"I'm *not* upset," I insisted. The phone rang, and I ran

into the kitchen. "Hanson residence, Merry speaking."

"Merry, hi!" It was Lissa.

"Hi." I sounded completely unenthusiastic.

"Are you busy?" There was that certain edge to her voice as if she was dying to tell me something, yet waiting politely for me to respond.

"Not really," I said, raising the pitch of my voice to ward off more questions. "What's up?"

"You'll never guess!"

I braced myself. "Guess *what?*"

"Oh, Merry, this is just too good to be true."

"What is?" My throat was already dry. I wished I hadn't asked.

"C'mon, Mer, you have to guess."

"Look, I don't feel like playing a guessing game right now, so either you tell me or you don't." I inched around the refrigerator, checking to see if Mom seemed interested in my end of the conversation.

Good! She was squatting down in front of the buffet, reaching for some serving dishes.

"Merry," Lissa said, sounding hurt. "What's wrong?"

"Nothing's wrong."

"You sound mad or something."

"Well . . . I'm not." I took a deep breath. "So, what were you saying?"

"It's about Jon Klein . . . and me."

My heart started beating ninety miles an hour. "Jon?" I managed to squeak out.

"And *me*," she said. "We're going to the eighth-grade picnic together—you know . . . at church."

I switched the phone to my left ear, hoping maybe I

32

hadn't heard correctly. "I . . . oh, that's nice."

"You'll never guess how he asked me," she continued.

I knew I'd probably seem like a real jerk if she kept talking and waiting for upbeat responses from me, but the truth was I wasn't happy for her. How could I be?

"Merry? You still there?"

"I've really gotta get going," I said.

"Okay, then," she said, almost giggling, "I'll talk to you later. 'Bye."

I didn't say goodbye. Just hung up the phone and stood there staring at it, refusing to cry.

"There we are," Mom said from the dining room as though I'd never even left to answer the phone. "Now for the roast and all the fixings."

She didn't even seem to notice the state I was in as she flounced through the kitchen, pulled out a drawer, and found a fancy apron to wear.

"I'm going for a walk," I said, attempting to make my voice sound normal. It cracked a little.

"Merry?" Mom turned to look at me. "What's wrong?"

"It's been a long week," I said, turning to leave.

Long wasn't the only thing the week—the day—had been. Long and lousy, both!

I thought of the Alliteration Wizard with a lump in my throat. Had Jon introduced Lissa to *our* word game? My heart sank at the thought. I hoped not. But then again, if he'd asked her out, maybe . . .

The sun beat down on me as I jogged the sloping stretch of road between our front lawn and SummerHill Lane, where the school bus always stopped. About a block away from my house, a dirt path led away from the road to a shortcut through the willow grove, to the Zook farm.

I kept running, feeling the anger rise in me.

Lissa and Jon. He'd asked her . . . not me.

My throat ached; the tears came. I ran harder, my red-and-white tennies pounding the ground. The path cut into the thick wild grass on either side as it headed into the dense, hidden part of the grove.

Faster and faster I ran. The distance from here to there seemed desperately long, not like it usually was when I came to visit Rachel. We would talk about the day, maybe have a slice of warm bread and her wonderful grape jelly. Sometimes she would show me a new pillow or doily she had made for her hope chest.

I made my legs move through the willow grove and down the pasture to the white picket fence. Through my tears, I could see Levi in the potato field, still working the mules. Levi—my childhood friend. Dear, fun-loving Levi.

I stopped crying. Catching my breath, I wiped my face on the tail of my red shirt and decided to stop in to see Rachel. This way, Levi would never have to know I'd been crying when I headed out to the field later.

"*Wilkom*, Merry." Rachel stepped out of the back door just as I came up the walk.

"Hi," I said. "I guess it's time for milking, right?"

"*Jah*." She wiped her hands on the long black apron covering her brown work dress. "Come help if you want."

Milking cows was one of my least favorite chores, especially the way Rachel and her family did it. And wiping down the cows' udders was the worst of it.

"I think I'll pass," I said. "Maybe I'll just take a walk and wait for you."

Rachel shielded her eyes with her hand as she looked at me. "Merry, is everything all right with you?"

"Don't mind me." I wondered if there were tear stains on my face. "Just thought I'd stop by and say hi."

She laughed. "Well, hi, then."

Abe Zook—her father—and Rachel's younger sisters, Nancy, Ella Mae, and little Susie, showed up outside the barn as if on cue. The whole family, except Levi and Mrs. Zook, was going to milk today.

"Guess you'd better get going," I told her. "I'll see you later."

"Sure you can't stay and help?" It was as if Rachel viewed the milking experience as something quite special.

"I'm sure, but thanks."

Rachel smiled her wide, energetic smile and scampered off barefoot to the barn.

Still wondering about my face, I hurried to the well pump a few feet away. I gave it a few good cranks and icy cold water poured out. The tin bucket caught the spillage, and I hurried over to dip my hand into the water, washing my face, especially my cheeks.

Now I was set.

I walked, ambling past the expanse of yard behind the old Zook farmhouse and the smaller addition built onto it called the *Grossdawdy Haus*, where Rachel's grandparents lived. On my far left was the long, earthen ramp that led up to the second story of the "bank barn." The hayloft was up there, and for an instant I was tempted to go and throw myself into the warm, sweet hay. But I kept going.

In spite of my day—in spite of Lissa's news—I had some truly good friends right here on SummerHill Lane. Rachel, a dear friend, full of cheer and always helpful. She'd even made a cross-stitch pillow for my hope chest. I guess she thought every girl had one.

And there was Levi, handsome and full of fun. As I walked through the potato field toward him, he pulled on the reins, bringing the mule team to a halt. With a wide grin he tipped his straw hat, and I almost forgot why I'd come.

"Merry!" he called from his perch. "It's good to see ya."

Maybe it was the way he stood there tall and confident with the dust and dirt of the day caked on his dark trousers and work shoes. Maybe it was the way his blue eyes twinkled when he smiled. I wasn't exactly sure why, but as I stood between the rows of potatoes, I didn't see the sense in setting Levi Zook straight about the phone call. About anything.

FIVE

"Did you call me today?"

Levi halted the mules. "I wondered if you'd like to go to the Green Dragon with me this Saturday."

"The Green Dragon?"

"They have soft pretzels and cotton candy." He paused. "It's like a carnival and—"

"I *know* what the Green Dragon is, Levi. But I'm not Amish, remember?"

His face clouded for a moment. "Well, I wish ya were," he said hesitantly. "It would make things easier."

"Not for me," I insisted, laughing. "I don't have to wash down the cows' you-know-whats before I can pour milk on my cereal."

The smile returned to his tan face. "That's not what I mean."

I wasn't going to ask what he *did* mean. After all, I wasn't completely ignorant—I'd seen this moment coming for years. "How are you getting to the Green Dragon?" I suspected he wasn't taking his courting buggy.

He glanced from side to side as though he was going to share something top secret. Then he pulled his wallet out.

"I just got a driver's license," he said, showing me.

"Levi, why?"

"Two of my cousins own a car," he whispered, quickly putting the card away. "We're in the same crowd together. We're called the Mule Skinners." He said it with pride.

I'd heard about the rambunctious Amish group. "Aren't they a little wild?"

He chuckled, carefree and easy. "A little barn dancin' never hurt anyone."

I sighed. "Well, there's a big difference between a barn hop and going out with an English girl."

Levi's face lit up. "Are you sayin' you'll come?"

"Well, I won't go if *you're* driving!" I was serious and he knew it. "Besides, your father will tan your hide if he catches you."

"Dat will never know."

"Well, if I were you, I'd ask an Amish girl instead."

He took his hat off suddenly. "But Merry, you're *not* me, so you don't understand." His eyes were more sincere than I'd ever seen them.

I felt awkward. Levi wasn't kidding. He really wanted me to go. "We have Sunday school and church early," I said, hoping to diffuse his eagerness. "I'd be tired if I was out late Saturday night."

"What about Sunday night?"

"Levi," I snapped, "what do you think my parents will say?"

He wasn't going to stand for any lecture from me. The women in his life were taught to be compliant and submissive. "Please, will ya listen?" He touched my arm lightly.

"No, I won't. Just because you're not baptized yet

doesn't mean you should push the rules. Your father's counting on you to follow in his footsteps."

I didn't really know that, not from Abe Zook directly, but it was the Amish way—passing the faith and culture from one generation to the next.

"I have plenty of time to decide about baptism," he said with conviction. "This is *my* life. Nobody else can live it for me."

In a strange sort of way, I understood.

"Well, what will your answer be?" he asked. "Will ya say 'Jah, *des kann ich du*'?"

Shielding my eyes from the afternoon sun, I looked up at him. "What's that supposed to mean—Jah, des kann . . . uh, whatever?"

"Just say, 'Yes, I will.' "

Even if I had wanted to go—and I wasn't sure I did—there was no way my parents would let me. "I'm really sorry, Levi."

He placed his straw hat back on his sweaty head, then picked up the reins and slapped the mules without speaking.

I thought I'd offended him by turning him down, and probably would've worried about it if I hadn't stayed for a moment longer.

To my surprise, when he reached the end of the row, Levi turned around and waved. "Maybe some other time. Jah?"

I have to admit I was relieved to see he was cheerful again. I waved back before going to find Rachel.

All the way to the barn, I thought of Levi. It seemed so strange, his interest in me. Sure, we went back a long way—to childhood days. And, yes, I'd saved him from drowning, but why wasn't he flirting with Amish girls after late-night singings like other Amish boys his age?

Why me?

∞   ∞

Supper that night was eaten by candlelight.

Everyone except Skip was seated at the table, made lovely by Mom's attention to lace, centerpiece, and polished silver. My brother had an appointment. At least that's what he said on his way out the back door before company arrived. But if you ask me, he was probably going out with Jon Klein's older sister. Again.

The roast and potatoes were baked to perfection, and Dad's cousins, Martin and Hazel, seemed pleased. Mom too.

Dad's relatives actually showed interest in my social studies assignment, although at first I thought they were only being polite.

Then Hazel mentioned something about her grandfather's journal. "You might want to include this tidbit of information in your project, Merry," she said, leaning forward and adjusting her glasses. "From what I understand, one of our ancestors, Joseph Lapp, was quite a fascinating fellow."

Dad agreed, chuckling. "One of the more interesting characters in our family tree."

I perked up my ears. "Was he the one who left the Amish?"

Dad nodded. "He's the black sheep of the family, I guess you'd say. Although"—he paused—"Hazel and I are his descendants, so I don't know where that puts us."

Mom smiled at Dad's remark.

Hazel's eyes brightened. "Weren't there some letters written by Joseph Lapp after the shunning?"

Dad nodded. "I'm not sure where they are, but it seems to me I have them packed away somewhere."

"Probably in the attic," Mom said, refolding her napkin and placing it under her dessert fork.

I had to know more about this shunning business. "Who were the letters written to?" I asked.

"I believe they were sent to Joseph's younger brother"— Dad glanced at the ceiling as though he was trying to put all this in perspective for me—"which would be your great-great uncle Samuel."

Hazel slid her glasses up her nose again. "Weren't the letters written during the six-week probation period before the actual shunning?"

"You know, now that you mention it, I think that's probably the case," Dad said.

Mom started clearing off the dinner plates. "Maybe you could locate the letters for Merry," she said.

"Oh, could you, Dad?" I pleaded.

He scratched his chin, looking rather nonchalant. "Well, I suppose so . . . if you'd like."

Like? I was delirious with the thought. "When can we do it?" I asked, ready to drop everything, candlelight dinner included.

Mom came in and filled the coffee cups, sending me a warning signal with her eyes. "I'm sure this can wait, Merry."

Cousin Hazel appeared to be as disappointed as I. But she didn't press the issue further, and all of us settled into a calm and quiet half hour of rhubarb pie, with black coffee for the adults.

I may have appeared to be calm and quiet, but I sure didn't feel that way. Dad's long-ago relative had left the Amish culture and gone through the *Bann* and *Meidung*.

Excommunication—the Bann—was bad enough, but not being allowed to eat or associate with his Amish relatives or friends in any way? Being disowned?

I wondered about Joseph Lapp. Who was he, really? And what made him leave?

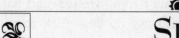
Later that night, Dad agreed to help me find the letters. "First thing tomorrow," he said before I headed off to bed.

Unfortunately, Saturday morning he was called away to the hospital before I got up, so I asked Mom where I should look.

"Try that old steamer trunk up in the attic." She stopped to think. "You might have to move some rugs to get to it."

"No problem," I said, scampering off to my parents' bedroom. Filled with anticipation, I opened the door leading to the attic.

Steep and solid, the attic steps were the original wood, as well-built and old as our hundred-year-old colonial frame house. The steps creaked, and I remembered the days when Faithie and I had played up here.

Years ago, Dad had succeeded in converting the drafty old place into an enchanting secret playroom simply by adding extra insulation and Sheetrock. Later, he painted the walls and put up oak trim around the gabled window. Next came bright and thick mauve carpet. Faithie loved the color. I didn't at first; it grew on me, though.

Now, the space had been turned into storage, and although boxes were stacked and color-coded in the far corner, the room still held its rustic charm.

Mom had kept all of Faithie's toys, dresses, and baby things, tenderly packing them away up here. The pain of loss had prompted Mom to save everything. She'd actually refused to part with any of it.

Two years had passed since I'd last set foot here. Staring at Faithie's childish art—drawings we'd hung on the walls—I realized once again how desperately I missed my twin.

The wind came up under the eaves, whistling a mournful tune, but there was no time for sadness now. I searched for the trunk Mom had mentioned and found it easily. Just as she had said, it was piled high with afghans and blankets wrapped in loose plastic, and Amish hook rugs by the dozen. With armloads of two or three at a time, I hauled them onto the floor, placing them carefully in a neat pile.

Then, slowly, carefully, I opened the giant lid. Peering into the enormous trunk, I saw all sorts of long-forgotten things.

One by one, I lifted small boxes out of the trunk, creating a semicircle of memories behind me on the floor. Then, almost unexpectedly, I noticed a sealed plastic bag wedged in between the wall of the trunk and another box. Taking care not to bend or disturb the contents, I pulled the plastic square out of its hiding place and into the light.

Old letters—at least five of them!

I studied the writing closely through the plastic. The name *Samuel Lapp* was visible in the center of the envelope, and although very faded, the gray ink was quite legible.

"Mom!" I sat at the top of the steep steps and scooted

down like Faithie and I had always done as little girls. "I found the letters!"

"In here, Merry," she called from her bedroom.

Excited, I dashed over to the wide window seat where she sat reading a book in the sunlight.

"Well"—she peered over her book—"why don't you have a look?"

"Do you think Dad'll mind if I read them before he gets back?"

She smiled wholeheartedly. "I doubt it—go ahead."

I sat on the edge of the antique four-poster bed, unsealed the plastic, and pulled out the stack of letters. "Wow," I whispered. "Can you believe this? These are *so* old."

Mom nodded. "Over a hundred years."

"It's like a blast from the past." I shivered. "O-oh, I feel like I'm beginning to tread on—"

"Merry," she interrupted, laughing. "You're dramatizing again."

"That's what Chelsea Davis says—constantly." I fingered the ancient envelopes, wondering more than ever about the life of Joseph Lapp—cast out by the Amish.

"Well, maybe it's good to have friends like Chelsea," Mom said, giving me her undivided attention for a change. "I guess all of us can use a little nudge toward reality now and then."

"Sure, Mom," I said, even though I had no idea what she was talking about.

I opened the first letter, careful not to tear the near-brittle, parchmentlike stationery. I scanned the page. The writing was foreign to me. My heart sank when I realized it was written in German.

"Something wrong?" Mom set her book aside.

I held up the letter. "Joseph Lapp spoke German, right?"

She threw her arms up. "Oh, of course!"

"Well, now what?" I said, more to myself than to Mom.

"Your father doesn't speak a word of it . . . never has."

"Wait a minute." I got up and went to the wide triple window overlooking the Zook farm. "I think I know someone who can translate these."

Mom swung her legs down off the cozy, pillowed perch. "Rachel might be able to decipher it, although she speaks a Pennsylvania Dutch dialect."

"I know," I said, "but she reads the Bible and other books in German."

Mom pointed to the letters lying on the bed. "Please take care of them. Your father didn't appear to be interested in this last night, but take my word for it, he would be mighty upset if the letters got lost."

"Count on me." I gathered the letters into the plastic once again and zipped them safely inside. "All set. Now I'm off to see Rachel."

"Not without breakfast, you aren't."

"Oh, Mom," I fussed.

Her eyes meant business. "Breakfast, Merry."

There was no way out of it. My mother had a hang-up about food. She truly believed a person had to eat heartily in order to stay healthy and productive. It was also the mentality of the plain people around us.

I sighed. Maybe the plain way of thinking was genetic—

got into the blood stream and worked its way to the brain. After all, if Grandfather Joseph with two greats in front of his name had been Amish, then surely *I* had some of that blood coursing through my veins, too.

I went to my room with the letters, placing them safely on top of my desk. Then I hurried down the back steps leading to the kitchen.

Mom encouraged me to eat. And eat. Finally, I held up my hands. "I'm full, honest!"

Skip grinned, accepting a third helping of fried eggs and ham. "You can't be full," he teased.

"Oh, yeah? Well, maybe *my* stomach hasn't stretched out as fat as yours."

He scowled. "Who said anything about fat?"

"That's what'll happen if you keep scarfing down everything in sight."

"Aw, how sweet," he said, taunting me. "Little Merry's looking out for her big brother." He reached over and tickled my elbow.

I jerked my arm away. "Quit picking on me!"

"Skip, please," Mom intervened. Then, eyeing me, she said, "Remember, Merry, your brother won't be around here next year."

"Hallelujah for college," I mumbled.

Skip laughed. "You'll miss me, little girl. You'll see."

"I can't wait to find out!" Pushing my chair back with a screech, I ran upstairs to brush my teeth.

What a relief, I thought. Starting next fall, I'd have Mom and Dad all to myself. Just like an only child . . .

Only child. That thought got me thinking about Lissa

Vyner, an honest-to-goodness only child—the last person I wanted to think about!

Eager to show Rachel the German letters, I gave my hair a quick brushing. Then I emptied my camera case, making room for Joseph Lapp's letters. I couldn't wait to find out more about this great-great grandfather of mine. Why *had* he abandoned his Amish life so long ago?

Staring at the letters, an anxious feeling crept over me. I remembered the words I'd said to Chelsea yesterday. *Don't all families have skeletons in their closets?*

I reached into the camera case and caressed the old letters. What secrets would I discover in my own family closet?

SEVEN

Rachel and Nancy Zook were helping their mother make *schnitz* pies when I arrived at their back door. My mouth watered as I smelled the delicious tartness of dried apples. Mm-m! Maybe I wasn't as full as I thought.

"Merry, it's good to see ya!" Rachel said, dropping everything to hurry to the screen door. "Come on in and sit for a spell."

I sat at the long wooden bench behind the equally long table in the spacious kitchen, observing the bustling activity. Rachel and her sister wore long dresses with black belted aprons pinned to their waists, and a *kapp*, a white netting head covering similar to their mother's.

"How many pies are you making?" I asked.

"Oh, seven or eight," Rachel replied. "The Yoders are having a quilting frolic. We're going over there later on to surprise them." She seemed very excited. "Sarah, my sister-in-law—you know, Curly John's wife—is expecting a baby in the fall."

"So you'll be an aunt for the first time?" I said.

Rachel noticed my camera case, but I quickly opened it, showing her it was empty except for the letters. The Amish

49

shied away from cameras because they believed the Bible told them not to make any graven images—photographs included.

"I wonder," I said, pulling the first letter out very carefully. "When you finish with the pies, could you read this to me?" I showed her the envelope, explaining my social studies project.

"Jah, this is German." She jabbered something quickly in Pennsylvania Dutch to her sister and mother while washing her hands, then dried them on her long black apron. "Come with me, cousin Merry."

I always grinned when she called me that, even though I'd been hearing it from her nearly all my life. Rachel Zook viewed me as her cousin, which I was. A very distant one.

We headed for the front porch, going through the wide dining room with a built-in corner cupboard where many fancy dishes were displayed. Next came the large, open living room. The Amish liked their living rooms uncluttered, without much furniture—a hickory rocking chair, hand-painted wooden chairs, and homemade throw rugs—so it was convenient to have church when it came their turn.

"The letters are very fragile." I gave the first one to Rachel. Her blue eyes were wide and she had a strangely curious expression.

"They even feel old, jah?" Rachel sat down on the old porch swing, sniffing the paper. "Smell old, too."

I leaned against the porch railing. "Very old."

She began to read under her breath as though she was trying to determine the content. "This is what Joseph Lapp wrote to his younger brother," she began, glancing at me with sincere eyes. " 'My dear brother and friend, Samuel

Lapp. It is with great sadness that I write these things. I can no longer live in the Amish community. I will miss you, my brother, and my sisters, too, and dear Mam and faithful Dat. With everything in me, I will miss all of you. It is not because of lack of love or respect for my family that I do this thing. It is for Mary . . . all for Mary, whom I plan to wed.' " Rachel stopped reading and sighed.

"Mary who?" I asked, eager for her to read on.

"Wait now," Rachel said, reading further silently. "He says something here about her being English—an outsider!" Rachel exclaimed. "He writes this: 'I love Mary deeply. I must be true to my heart and make her my wife.' "

Rachel stared at the letter for a moment longer, not reading. Her face turned suddenly pale. "Ach, *der gleh Deihenger*—so this is the little scoundrel!"

"What are you saying?"

"This man, this Joseph Lapp—your relative—is the same shunned man Grossdawdy has been telling us about for many years. He has set Joseph Lapp up as an example of wickedness for as long as I can remember."

"Because of the shunning?" I said softly.

She nodded. "And because my own brother, Levi, is every bit as headstrong as Joseph Lapp was." She glanced around as if it was something she shouldn't be saying.

I rushed over and sat beside Rachel, gazing at the letter, then at her. "Your grandfather has heard stories about Joseph Lapp?" I whispered. "Wow. This is heavy."

Rachel frowned. "Heavy?"

"Surprising," I restated my words.

"Surprising to you, but shameful to me."

"For you, Rachel? How?"

She nodded, solemnly. "This man"—and here she tapped the letter—"was one of *my* ancestors, too."

"So *that's* the connection between us," I said. "I always wondered how we were distant cousins." I glanced at my watch, then at the letters. "Will you read the rest to me sometime?"

"Jah, sometime."

"Thank you, Rachel." I paused, studying my friend. "I never meant to upset you."

"I'll be fine." But her eyes looked sad.

"I better get going. I've heard enough to get started on my school project. You've been a big help." I stood up to leave, eager to get started working with Chelsea.

Rachel handed the letters back to me. "Just ask if you need more help," she volunteered, following me down the front porch steps.

"I hope your schnitz pies turn out extra good," I said, trying to get her mind off the sorrowful thoughts. "Please tell Curly John that Skip and I said hi. I'm sure he'll make a very good father."

She broke into a smile. "I will, Merry. And may God go with you."

I waved before leaving, feeling sorry about stirring up sad feelings in my friend. And yet I wondered about Rachel's emotional reaction to the letter. Why had this story been told so often in the Zook household? Was it really because of Levi?

I flew through the pasture, over the white picket fence, and into the willow grove. Out of breath, I stopped for a moment in the dense, thick part—Faithie's and my old secret place, now where Rachel and I often shared secrets.

Secrets . . .

Right then, standing in the middle of the trees with summer green sheltering me and sunlight twinkling around me, I remembered Levi Zook's words. *I wish you were Amish, Merry. It would make some things much easier.*

Knowing that Levi had heard the story of his rebellious ancestor at the knee of his grandfather since childhood, I wondered exactly what he meant.

That's when the realization hit me. Hit me between the eyes as I stood in the wispy willows on the dividing line between the Zooks' Amish farm and my own home. I, Merry Hanson, might very well have been Amish had it not been for Joseph Lapp!

EIGHT

Chelsea Davis was waiting for me in her backyard when I arrived.

I'd gone around the house and through the brick walkway when no one answered the front door. There, amidst elaborate flower beds arranged in lovely designs, I found her sitting on a padded lawn chair just under the shade of a patio umbrella. She was wearing her favorite shorts outfit from last summer.

Chelsea was sketching her family tree on a long, vertical piece of art paper, her hair pulled back in a single, thick braid.

I cleared my throat, and she looked up, somewhat surprised. "Nobody came to the front door," I said, explaining my unannounced appearance. "I thought it was okay to come around."

She stretched and smiled. "Is it one-thirty already?"

I nodded. "Actually, I'm a little late."

"Better late than never." She laughed. "Pull up a chair."

"Thanks." I pulled out the lawn chair next to her, away from the glass patio table. Taking my time, I spread out the background information on several relatives, including Joseph Lapp.

"Hey, no fair. Looks like you're half done with your project," she teased.

"How far are you?"

She held up her family tree, clearly sketched with long lines drawn straight and neat under each set of branches. "I'm not sure how far back I can go . . . or want to go," she said, glancing over her shoulder toward the house.

"How come?"

Chelsea's mind seemed to wander. "Well, from what my mom says, there've been some really weird types floating around in the branches of our family tree."

I smiled. "Really? Couldn't be any weirder than anyone else's family."

"Oh, yeah?" She crossed her legs Indian fashion beneath her and leaned forward. "I told you I'd rather go bungee jumping over sharks."

I nodded, not believing her. "So, what could be so weird?"

"You won't freak out if I tell you?" she asked, looking serious.

"Why should I? It's *your* family."

"I take it that's a promise," she said without cracking a smile.

"Sure, whatever."

Holding up her sketch, Chelsea pointed to a double branch three lines above her own name. "Right here." She pointed. "This is my great aunt Essie Peterson."

"Really? You're related to *her?*"

Chelsea's green eyes widened in horror. "You mean you know about her?"

"Doesn't everyone?" I said.

She scrunched up her face, looking deflated. "But Essie was so strange."

I wondered if Chelsea's great-aunt was the reason why my friend fought off all my comments about God.

"Check this out." She reached for her spiral notebook lying on the glass table across from me. "Essie was my grandfather's sister on my dad's side. She had healing meetings where sick people came from all over. People said she had some kind of power, I guess."

"From God, right?"

"Well, from something." Chelsea laughed. "She'd go without eating, sometimes for several days before her so-called healing meetings. My dad said the way he heard it, Essie was tuned in and turned on—like a charge of electricity."

"And people got well, right?"

She nodded, pushing a stray wisp of hair back over her ear. "That's the weirdest part, I guess. People showed up sick and went away just fine." She paused, that faraway look returning. "How do you figure?"

I saw my opportunity, and with a silent prayer for wisdom, I forged ahead. "Remember the martyrs we were talking about it yesterday? Well, the same God who softened the last terror-filled minutes of their lives . . . that same God gave his Son power to heal people. And just before Jesus went back to heaven, He told His disciples that they'd do even greater things than He had. I know it sounds truly amazing, but it's all in the Bible."

"Well, forget it then. I don't believe all that nonsense." She went back to her sketching.

Why does she always do that? I thought. I couldn't get a grasp of this recurring problem. It seemed as though Chelsea allowed herself to get only so close to the gospel and then—*Bam!* she'd cut herself off from it.

Disappointed, I refused to be sucked into her little game. On again. Off again. I could only hope that every talk we had about God really was leading Chelsea slowly but surely to Him. Because as frustrating as she was, the grandniece of the late Essie Peterson was a precious soul in God's eyes.

We moved on to other topics, but the idea that she'd have to divulge her connection to this woman of God in front of the entire social studies class really seemed to bug her.

When I asked her about it, Chelsea was firm, not embarrassed.

"People like me shouldn't have relatives like Essie Peterson."

"Really?" I decided to tone things down, hoping to open the door again.

She exhaled loudly. "You'd think that somewhere in my genetic makeup there oughta be someone like me . . . somewhere way back there." She waved her hand "You know, someone who thought all this God business was for the birds."

I thought of referring to the scriptures I knew about God's care of even the smallest sparrow, but didn't. "Do your parents believe in God?" I asked.

She blew air through her mouth in disgust. "I wish I

knew what my parents believed these days."

I didn't want to touch that remark, so I kept listening, looking at her.

"Mom's into some bizarre stuff," she said. "I don't think *she* even knows for sure what it is. Her assortment of crystals seems to be growing by the hour. She even has a mood ring, whatever that is."

Sounded like the occult to me. "What about your dad?" I asked in a hushed voice.

"Oh, he reads all these books on past lives and what he thinks he'll come back as next. None of it makes any sense." She reached up, stretching, her fingers almost touching the edge of the patio umbrella.

"You're right, it doesn't."

"Hey, good. You're not going to preach." She looked so confident perched there on her lawn chair.

I wanted to tell her that what her parents were getting into was dangerous. Instead, I said, "No preaching, Chelsea, but I won't stop caring about you."

For a moment, I thought I saw her eyes glisten, but she looked away, and not wanting to stare, so did I.

NINE

After breakfast Sunday morning, I looked in my dresser mirror, watching my shoulder-length hair flip from side to side as I tried to air dry it a little before using the blower.

Staring at my eyes, I wondered about Joseph Lapp. Was he brown eyed, too?

I smiled into the mirror. Did he ever wish for the ability to take pictures, long before instamatic cameras?

Glancing at my wall gallery, I focused on the tall picture of a lone willow tree. Did Grandfather Joseph ever contemplate his life out among the trees and beside the river the way I often did?

It wasn't fun being left in the dark about someone so fascinating. Or as Rachel said, a scoundrel. But was Joseph Lapp a wicked man, really?

The silence started to bug me, or I should say, the *questions* I was asking myself without any hope of answers bugged me. I turned on the blow dryer to fill the silence.

Lily White jumped off the bed and darted over to me. "You wanna go to Sunday school, huh?" I leaned down and picked her up with my free hand, nuzzling her against my damp hair, letting the blower tickle her white coat. She arched her back and let out a long hiss, so I put her down. "I suppose we'll just have to wait and see what happens with Lissa and Jon today at church," I told her, even though she seemed more interested in sulking under my bed. "They'll probably be sitting together, you know."

I braced myself with that discouraging thought.

"Merry?" Mom poked her head in the door.

I shut off the blower.

"I heard you talking." She glanced around.

"Oh, I was just having a chat with Lily White. She's not very interested, as you can see."

Mom inched her way into the room. "Is everything all right?"

"Why shouldn't it be?"

She shook her head. "Well, I don't know. I just haven't heard you sound so depressed like this."

"Like what?" I demanded. "What did you hear?"

She stood beside me, looking in the mirror at the two of us. "There was a time when you could tell me anything, remember?" She slipped her arm around my waist.

I was silent.

"I miss those days." She gave me a little squeeze.

Frustrated and upset that she'd probably overheard me mention Lissa and Jon, I felt my muscles stiffen against her. "Do you think Dad could tell me more about Joseph Lapp sometime today?"

Mom stepped back out of the mirror's reflection. "Why don't you ask him?" Her face clouded.

I hadn't responded to her plea for intimacy, and she was hurt. I'd turned the tables and requested an audience with my dad—instead of her.

"Well, we'd better get moving." She turned to leave. "You know how your father is on Sundays."

Dad was a stickler for promptness, especially Sundays. He was a fanatic about leaving the house on time. I chafed under the time pressure, and to speed things up, I turned my hair dryer on the highest setting. The strong heat would make my hair frizzy, but it was better than a tongue lashing from Dad.

❧   ❧

I can't begin to recount the happenings of my day at church. Here it was already May 14, close to the end of the school year, and every girl in the youth class was sitting with a guy.

Honestly, I felt like an alien from another planet. It wasn't so much embarrassing as it was ridiculous. Why did everyone wait until the end of the school year to pair off?

I scanned the room. As I'd predicted, Lissa and Jon sat together across the room. I purposely chose a place where I wouldn't see them every time I looked at Mrs. Simms, our super-cool teacher.

Repeat performance for church an hour later. It seemed that Lissa had abandoned her mother to sit with Jon in the Klein family pew. Jon's older sister, Nikki, had her eyes on Skip, however, as I slid into the pew next to him several rows back.

I had no idea what Nikki Klein saw in my cat-queasy brother. Skip was good looking enough, I guess—for a brother anyway. Tall with golden brown hair and hazel eyes that sparkled sometimes. But if Nikki *really* knew him—the way I did—she'd probably run the other way. Fast!

I scarcely heard the pastor's sermon, even though I truly wanted to. The sight of Lissa and Jon sitting together kept distracting me. Jon Klein looked absolutely delighted sitting there with Lissa at his side. Completely crushed, I wondered if he'd introduced her to the word game yet. And if so, could she keep up with him the way I always had?

As best I could, I avoided them after the service by simply hanging around my parents. Dad seemed happy with the extra attention I gave him on the way down the aisle and out to the parking lot. To my delight, he agreed to tell me more about Joseph Lapp.

"We'll talk right after dinner," he said, holding the car door open for Mom.

After a spectacular spread of baked chicken, mashed potatoes, gravy, yellow buttered squash, peas and carrots, and a whole series of "No thank-yous" when I felt too stuffed to move, Mom shooed Dad and me into the living room.

Skip helped with the kitchen at her request. I was surprised he didn't give her a hard time about it. Maybe being a high-school senior was doing him some good. If I could just get him to accept my cats as part of the family . . .

Dad settled down in his easy chair to tell his tales. "To begin with, your grandfather Hanson, my father, was as sharp as a tack when it came to remembering passed-down details and events. So I guess you could say I have him to thank for the stories about Joseph Lapp."

I sat on the end of our green paisley sofa, sharing the matching ottoman with Dad, intent on what he was about to say.

"Joseph Lapp, I was told, had a rebellious streak in him from the day he was born," Dad said.

I thought of Levi Zook's grandfather, who had pounded away at the stories of Joseph Lapp's rebellion and consequences.

Dad continued. "Evidently, Joseph was the last to be baptized in his family, and even then, he broke his vow by marrying outside the church."

"What did he look like?" I asked.

Dad moved a tasseled throw pillow out from behind him. "As a matter of fact, he was tall and lanky, had a full head of light brown hair, and the bluest eyes this side of the Pocono Mountains."

The description matched Levi Zook perfectly.

"Sounds like someone I know," I replied.

"Well, plenty of Amishmen match that description, I suppose." He leaned back. "But not many do what Joseph Lapp did, at least not back in those days."

"What do you mean?" I was all ears.

"Being ousted from the church—that's excommunication. An Amishman's life revolves around the community of men and women who make up the church district. They fill one another's silos and plow or milk when a farmer is too sick or has no sons. They pitch in money to take care of one another during drought or hard times. They rejoice when new babies are born, and they mourn and bury their dead together." Dad paused, sighing. "The key word to remember about the Amish is *community*."

I crossed my legs on the ottoman. "If a person is kicked out of the community, how does he survive?"

Dad's eyes grew more serious. "Many Amish who leave return often because of the hardship of shunning."

"Something like being disowned, right?"

He nodded. "Not only does the person lose close ties with his family, he isn't allowed to eat or do business with *any* of his Amish relatives or friends. It must surely seem like a death to the loved ones involved. But if it weren't for the shunning, lots of young Amish teens would leave the church for cars and electricity."

"Do you think Joseph Lapp ever repented?"

"Well, if he had, you and I might be sitting in the middle of a group of Amish folk right now, finishing up Sunday dinner," Dad said with a weak smile and then a hearty yawn.

I could see he was tired. Sunday was the one day out of the whole week he wasn't on call, and he wasn't getting any younger. In fact, this summer Dad would celebrate his fiftieth birthday.

I gave him a hug before covering him with one of Mom's many afghans. Then I giggled looking at him lying there. "Just think, by now, if we were Amish, your beard would be down to here." I pointed to my stomach.

"Very funny, Merry," he said.

Hurrying upstairs, I wrote down everything I could remember about Joseph Lapp, wondering why he'd married outside the Amish church.

After that, I went to Dad's study and was closing the door when I turned around and discovered Skip there on the phone. He gave me one of his get-lost looks.

"For how long?" I whispered.

He said, "Excuse me for one sec, Nikki," covering the phone as his eyes squinted into narrow little slits.

I stood my ground. "I need the phone."

"Wait outside," he barked. "And shut the door when you leave."

"How much longer?"

"You're really making this difficult, you know?" Skip glared at me.

"I'll give you five minutes. If you're not off the phone by then, look for me in your room raiding your desk drawer."

Skip's eyes bulged. "You wouldn't dare!"

"Five minutes." I turned and walked out, leaving the door wide open. His gasps of exasperation were obvious as I scurried down the hall, suppressing a giggle.

Precisely seven minutes passed. I headed directly for my brother's room. The door was partway open, so I barged in, heading for his desk.

Not everyone knew my brother kept a journal. It seemed like a girl thing to do, but he really enjoyed keeping a record of his life. So did I, in a more unusual way—by photographing people, places, and things.

I slid his chair away from the desk, making sure it screeched across the hardwood floor. That way Skip would know I meant business, since his bedroom was directly above Dad's study.

Listening, I smiled. The unmistakable sound of footsteps could be heard on the stairs.

Genius!

I made a mad dash out of Skip's room and down the hall to my bedroom. With my heart pounding ninety miles an hour, I locked the door.

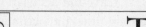

TEN

"What were you doing in my room?" Skip bellowed through my door.

I giggled at his reaction. "I gave you fair warning."

"I'm telling Mom!"

"Go ahead, tattle baby."

I heard the pounding of his big feet on the back stairs that led down to the kitchen. But as fast as he left, he returned, thumping his fist against my door.

"Where's Mom?" he demanded.

"Probably out for her afternoon stroll, dear brother," I said, sprinkling my words with a British accent.

"Cut the Princess Di routine," he sneered. "You're dead meat for this."

"What did *I* do?"

He stomped around outside my door. "Did you snoop at anything?" There was a twinge of desperation in his voice.

Good. Maybe this would give me some leverage for later. If and when I needed it.

"So," I began snootily, "it's you and Nikki, is it?"

"When are you ever going to keep your nose out of other people's business?"

I let him rant on and on while I reclined on my bed, stroking my four cats. The door seemed to heave and sway with the noise of his meaningless threats and accusations.

When I didn't comment for a long time, he insisted that I answer. I remained silent, laughing under my breath that I'd never even touched his precious desk drawer. Or journal. Finally, he evaporated—the weirdest brother a girl could ever have.

When I knew he was back in his room, probably recounting his most recent romantic chat for his journal, I crept down the hall, past his door to the steps.

Downstairs, I found peace and solitude in Dad's study as I talked on the phone to Chelsea. When I hung up, Lissa called.

"Hi, Mer," she said all pert and sweet.

I curled my toes. She was the last person on earth I wanted to talk to. "How's your family tree growing?" I said.

She laughed. "Very clever."

I held my breath, afraid she'd say, *Say that with all c's.*

"Chelsea and I got most of ours done yesterday," I said.

"Jon and I are nearly finished, too," she said.

More than anything, I wished *that* were true. Finished as in kaput—over!

Lissa continued. "I can't wait for the eighth-grade picnic. It'll be really cool. You're going, aren't you?"

"Not sure." If she and Jon were going, there was no way I'd be showing up.

"Why don't you ask someone?" She sounded all excited. "Then the four of us could go together!"

Oh no! This was truly horrible.

"We'll see," I said, gritting my teeth.

70

"Don't wait too long," she advised. "The picnic's only twelve days away."

"I'll remember that."

"Well, I'd better get going. See ya." We hung up.

Frustrated, I went to do math homework, trying not to think my depressing thoughts. It wasn't easy. Lissa was wild about Jon; there was no getting past that. But how interested was Jon in *her*?

❧   ❧

I finished my algebra in record time, then headed to the garage to get my bike, securing my camera case and water bottle in the bike basket before pushing off.

I wondered if I'd see Mom out walking, but I knew she usually went *up* the hill toward Strawberry Lane. I was going down SummerHill to the covered mill bridge several miles from here. Besides, I needed to be alone.

It was a good long distance to pedal, but the exercise wasn't the only factor. Hunsecker's Mill Bridge was beautiful any time of year, but especially in late spring. A truly peaceful place to contemplate life's disappointments . . . among other things.

The afternoon was humid, but a mild breeze rippled the grass in the ditch beside the dirt road. Birds sang heartily as I followed the banks and curves on SummerHill Lane toward the main road. I suspected an afternoon shower—the birds seemed to know these things first—although there was little indication from the sky. A perfect deep blue, and only a few thunderclouds in the distance.

Everywhere I looked, flowers were beginning to push their heads up, adding a colorful addition to my ride and a fragrant touch to the air. Summer was almost here!

I stopped by the side of the road to take a picture of Mrs. Fisher's flowers. Profuse with dark pink peonies, the lovely flower garden was framed by two lilac bushes, one on each side. Carefully, I set my camera for the proper lighting and distance, then snapped away, hoping at least one of the shots would capture the brilliance.

Just then Ben Fisher, the oldest son, came outside. "Hello, Merry!" He sat on the front step.

I smiled. "Don't worry, I didn't get you in the picture."

"That's good. I've been in enough trouble for a spell." He exchanged a somber look with his elderly father, who sat in a hickory rocking chair nearby, puffing on a pipe.

I snapped my camera case shut and waved goodbye, wondering how Ben Fisher was doing. He'd dabbled with the modern world for a while—sowed some wild oats as the Amish say—even bought a car and had an English girlfriend. But Levi Zook, his true and loyal friend, had helped bring him back into the Amish community.

Last I heard, Ben gave a kneeling confession in front of the local church district not long ago. All was forgiven. I wondered if Levi and Ben were still good friends—and if so, why was Levi running with a crowd like the Mule Skinners?

I hurried down the road, eager for the tranquil setting of the Conestoga River and the old covered bridge. Pedaling hard, I flew down SummerHill to the intersection at Hunsecker Mill Road.

Minutes later, I arrived at the bridge. I got off my bike and pushed it through the deep, wild grass along the south side. Locating a tree, I abandoned my wheels, and with camera and water bottle in tow, headed for the quiet banks of the river.

There, in the partial shade of a giant maple, I settled down for some serious photo shooting. First, I took several shots of the bridge itself, finding the most unique angle possible for my scrapbook. Next came the river and the large, stately trees and flowering bushes. What a glorious day!

I put my camera away and sat there, listening to the sounds of springtime as the midafternoon light cast curious shadows over the water. I wondered what it would be like to have someone fall in love with me. Really, and truly in love.

Oh, I'd formed some ethereal ideas about it, of course, but never anything concrete. Maybe he'd paint my name on a billboard somewhere. Maybe he'd hire a sky painter. And there was always the Goodyear blimp . . .

I daydreamed about the endless possibilities. And by doing so, forced the discouraging thoughts of Jon Klein out of my mind.

Down the road to the east, I heard hoofbeats. Fast, clippity-clopping ones. Soon the horse and buggy came into view. For a fleeting moment, I envied the young couple in the open courting buggy, until I saw there was only a lone boy in the buggy. Light brown bangs peeked out of his black, wide-brimmed hat.

I stood up, trying to get a better look.

The buggy made the turn into the bridge. Pounding hoofbeats rattled the loose boards inside. Was it my imagination, or had the driver increased his speed? It sounded like the wild, reckless way Levi Zap 'em Zook handled his horse.

I sat back down in the grass, ducking my head, hoping Levi wouldn't see me. If it *was* Levi.

"Merry!" came his voice. "I know you're over there."

I popped up like I'd been shot out of a canon. "Hi, Levi," I called to him. "What are you doing here?"

"I should ask you the same question, jah?" He tipped his hat flirtatiously.

My brain was definitely out of commission, but I must not have been aware of it then. I stooped to pick up my water bottle and camera case and proceeded to walk over to the road. To Levi.

"Well, now, Merry, wouldja care for a lift home?" he asked, glancing heavenward. As if on cue, a thunderclap made me jump.

"I . . . uh, better not. But thanks," I said, gazing at his beautiful, black buggy.

"It's all right, Merry. Honest." He leaned forward, his foot on the rim, extending his hand to me. I had to admit he looked handsome in his Sunday best. Very handsome, now that I thought about it. What *was* I thinking?

Hesitant, I asked, "What if someone sees you with me? Won't you be in trouble?"

He laughed, suddenly displaying an umbrella. "Not for being neighborly."

I smiled. He had a point.

"What about my bike?" I glanced over my shoulder.

"Easy as pie," he said. "It'll fit." And he jumped down and went with me to retrieve it.

"Well, I guess you win this time," I said.

When my bike was finally situated, Levi helped me into the front of his buggy. I sat beside him to his left and caught the scent of sweet aftershave. Had he planned this encounter? Had he seen me leave my house earlier?

Feeling shy, I looked down and noticed the slate gray wall-to-wall carpeting on the floor. A large speedometer attached to a mini-dashboard on the right side was planted directly in front of Levi.

Quickly, he opened the umbrella. "It's starting to rain," he said, holding it over our heads with one hand.

I glanced at the dark sky from my sheltered perch, still surprised that I'd allowed myself to do this. "Thanks for the ride," I said for courtesy's sake and no other. Yet, I felt safe and protected next to Levi. Nothing like the way I thought it would be riding in an Amish courting buggy on a rainy Sunday.

Levi turned to face me under our private canopy. "I've been waiting a long time for this, Merry." The serious look in his eyes took me off guard.

Then, gallantly, he picked up the reins with his other hand and *gently* trotted his bold and beautiful Belgian horse up the road toward SummerHill.

ELEVEN

All the way up Hunsecker Mill Road we talked. And there was plenty of time for it. The pace of horse and buggy transportation wasn't exactly speedy at twelve miles per hour—and that was pushing it.

Under the menacing rain clouds, Levi and I talked about everything. I never realized how much we had in common. He truly loved nature. He appreciated the beauty of the earth-brown soil, the golden corn tassels, and the blue of his alfalfa field—together creating a colorful patchwork quilt.

"Have ya seen the mint leaves growing over in the meadow behind the barn?" Levi asked, full of questions. "Have ya seen the sun setting behind the Yoders' tobacco shed?"

I waited till the flow of questions stopped. "It's going to be a beautiful summer," I said at last.

"Jah," he agreed. "It could be a *wonderful-gut* summer." He slowed the horse from a trot to a leisurely walk, still holding the umbrella over our heads.

I wondered why we were slowing down.

"Merry," he said, turning to me. "I want to know something."

My hands felt clammy in my lap.

Levi didn't smile as he spoke. "I like ya, Merry. Always have."

I gave a soft little laugh, remembering our childhood pranks. The rope swing in the hayloft. The fun of growing up next to a houseful of Amish kids. "We've been good friends for a long time. You *already* know me," I said.

"But I must know your true answer."

"To what?"

Levi pulled on the reins with his free hand, halting his horse right there in the middle of the road. "I must ask a question." He paused a second, studying me. "Merry, will ya be my girl?"

Any other time I would've been shocked, taken off guard. But here, sharing our interests and talking freely the way we had, his question seemed like a semi-reasonable request.

His eyes were sincere and made me feel shy. I responded by looking down at my lap, speechless.

"Merry?" His voice pursued me.

"I'll have to think about it."

"Don't think *too* hard."

I looked up slowly. "There's a lot to think about, Levi. For one thing, you're Amish. Remember what happened to your friend Ben Fisher?"

He shrugged. "Ben did some terrible awful things, but you . . . you and me, we're friends from long past."

"Still, how could you think of dating an English girl?" It

was the old argument. The one I'd brought up two days ago in the potato field.

"I'm not thinking of dating an English girl." His face broke into a broad grin. "I want to spend time with *you*."

"And I'm English." I sighed.

"I will be busy working the farm this summer, ya know. There won't be much time for—"

"What are you saying?"

"Amish boys see their girls every other Saturday night and sometimes after Sunday night singings. They go for a long drive, and then head home sometime before dawn."

I leaned back, giving him an honest-to-goodness straightforward look. "Oh, so *that's* it." I laughed. "You intend to hide me under the stars."

He grinned. "We always keep such things secret. That's our way. I would not hide ya purposely from the view of my parents."

I understood. All of Amish dating and courtship was conducted under the covering of night. No one ever really knew who an Amish boy was seeing until the *Schteckliman* or go-between verified an engagement of marriage with the bride-to-be and her parents. Levi and his people had been courting the same way for three hundred years.

"But what would happen if you were seen with me?" I asked, still curious about Levi's willingness to risk being caught.

"It won't happen," he said firmly.

"And if it did?"

Levi let the reins drop over his right knee. He steadied the umbrella with both hands, leaning close to me. "I am not certain about my future as an Amishman," he said, almost in a whisper. "Baptism into the church would change everything for me, Merry. For now, I am free to decide, don'tcha see?"

This was serious talk. I felt uneasy hearing Levi discuss his uncertainties. "What about the girls in your crowd?" I asked. "Won't they wonder why you're not asking them out?"

Levi picked up the reins with his right hand, still holding the umbrella over my head. "There are no Amish girls for me, Merry." He looked away, suddenly paying more attention to the road ahead.

A car was coming in the opposite lane, and for the first time since I'd consented to ride with Levi, I felt nervous. Worried for him, I slouched a bit, hoping the driver wouldn't see me.

The red sports car sped past us, and I felt a light spray. The rain had stopped beating down on us now, but the road glistened from the afternoon shower. A gentle drizzle made the ride in Levi's buggy even more enchanting.

Suddenly, I realized who the red car belonged to. Miss Spindler—Old Hawk Eyes herself!

My throat went dry thinking about the nosy neighbor who lived behind my house. If she had spotted me with Levi just now, we were as good as published on the front page of the *Lancaster New Era!*

"I could leave the Sunday singin' early and come get-cha," Levi was saying.

"Only if I agree to it."

He nodded solemnly, playing along with me.

Then I giggled, thinking about the snazzy red sports car

and its owner. "That was Miss Spindler back there, in case you didn't know."

"Ach, she's harmless," he said. "What good would it do for her to tell on us?"

"Oh, you might be surprised. Old Hawk Eyes lives for the opportunity to spy on her neighbors."

A chuckle escaped Levi's lips. "Well then, our problem is solved, isn't it?"

I was totally confused. "What problem?"

"If she saw us, then everything's already out in the open." His eyes were shining. "No more worries. Jah?"

"Maybe not for you." I shook my head, thinking about Mom and Dad. What would *they* think if I consented to date an Amish boy?

TWELVE

When we approached the dirt lane leading to the Zook farm, I asked Levi to let me out. "Thanks for the ride," I said, eyeing the speedometer on his makeshift dashboard. There was no question in my mind that he would've zipped down SummerHill if I hadn't accepted the ride.

"I hope I'll see ya again soon," he said, bringing the horse to a stop.

"If the rains keep coming, maybe you will," I joked, glancing at the sky. "I would've been soaked if you hadn't come."

He leaped into the back of the buggy to unload my bike. "Will ya give me your answer soon, Merry?"

"I'll think about it," I said, even though I had no idea what on earth I would decide.

"Okay, then," he said, smiling to beat the band. "I'll say goodbye."

"Bye, Levi. And thanks again."

He sprang up into his buggy, lifted the reins, and sped toward his house. I giggled as I hopped on my bike. Zap 'em Zook was showing off again.

After I arrived home, I finished the remaining work required for my family history by making several phone calls to local relatives. It was actually fun doing the phone interviews, and since it was Sunday, most everyone was home and eager to chat about their life, reciting dates and details.

I was surprised that nearly all my Hanson relatives had heard about Joseph Lapp and his shunning.

Later, Mom gave me permission to call her sister long distance. Because Aunt Teri was deaf, I knew I'd be talking to Uncle Pete. He would sign the questions to his wife and she'd sign her responses back to him.

"Hello?" he answered the phone.

"Hi, Uncle Pete. This is your niece in Pennsylvania."

"Well, how's merry Merry doing these days?" He always said my name twice.

"I'm fine, thanks." I explained that I was working on an assignment for school.

"Family trees, eh?" he said. "Well, we're adding two more branches to *our* tree very soon." Aunt Teri was expecting twins the end of June. Both she and Uncle Pete were counting the days.

"How's Aunt Teri feeling?" I asked.

"She has to rest a lot, but other than that, real fine."

"I was wondering if Aunt Teri could answer some questions for my school project."

"Let me check." Uncle Pete went to find Aunt Teri. Soon he returned. "I'm sorry, but your aunt's sleeping soundly. Why don't you give the questions to me, and I'll jot them down and call you back tomorrow evening."

"Okay, thanks," I said.

One by one, I read my list of questions. When I finished,

I thanked him for taking the time. "Let us know when the babies come."

"We certainly will."

I felt awkward, unsure of what to say next. Then I blurted, "Have you picked out names yet?"

The idea of having twin cousins seemed strange to me. Actually, I felt a total reluctance toward another set of twins in the family. Maybe I was hesitant for other reasons. Maybe I was afraid the advent of twin babies would stir up suppressed memories of Faithie, neatly tucked away like her dresses and toys and things in the attic playroom.

Uncle Pete laughed, robust and jolly. "Oh, we're still throwing names around. Any suggestions?"

Honestly, I hadn't given it a single thought. Didn't really care to, but I would never let on. My lack of enthusiasm might hurt Uncle Pete. "Maybe you should wait till after they're born to see what names fit them."

"That's a terrific idea." He continued to chuckle in the midst of our goodbyes.

I hung up the phone and sat there in Dad's study, staring into space. *Lord, help me accept Aunt Teri's twin babies*, I prayed silently. *Maybe it would help if you'd let them turn out to be boys.*

As for Levi Zook, I had no idea what to pray. I'd promised to give him an answer. What on earth was I thinking, accepting a ride in his buggy? I'd probably never live it down. He would take it as a good sign—that maybe I was actually thinking of accepting his invitation.

I thought back to the afternoon I'd spent with Levi. We'd discussed many things. And surprise surprise, I had more in common with him than I'd ever dreamed.

Sitting back against the comforting fabric of Dad's desk chair, I daydreamed about my bike ride to the covered bridge, the quiet moments on the riverbanks, the pictures I'd taken . . . and the more I relived the day, the more I realized something. Something quite disturbing, actually. I *liked* Levi Zook.

I liked his rambunctious, carefree way. The way he could go from driving his buggy recklessly through the covered bridge with the staccato-sound of rumbling boards, to trotting his horse home in a gentle mist of a leftover shower. With a modern girl at his side.

The boy was truly unconventional. He seemed to know what he wanted and went after it. And he was stubborn. Persistent, too. Which reminded me of Joseph Lapp, who must've had some of the same personality traits.

Dad came into the room, and I popped out of my daydreaming. He looked refreshed after a long nap.

"Feeling better?" I asked.

"Forty winks can make a big difference." He ran his fingers through his graying hair and yawned.

I almost brought up the subject of Levi Zook, but chickened out and showed him my phone interviews for Social Studies instead.

"Come to think of it, we might have a book of family crests around here." He surveyed his book shelf.

"That'd be great."

He searched for the book, then located it. "Here we are." He thumbed through the pages to the 1918 Hanson coat of arms. On the page was a full-color picture of the crest, a lion holding an antler in its forepaw was the focal point.

"Looks like the name Hanson spells courage," Dad said proudly.

"Mind if I borrow this to make my sketch?"

"Help yourself."

"Thanks, Dad." I skedaddled off to my room to work on the artistic part of my project.

Lily White rubbed against my leg as I sat at my desk trying to concentrate. Finally, after persistent meowing from my cuddly kitten, I picked her up. "What do you want, baby?" She began to purr as I nuzzled her face with my hand.

"How's this for attention?" I propped a small pillow under her and she curled up contentedly on my desk. "Wanta know a secret?" I whispered, putting my face down close to hers.

She closed her eyes halfway.

"Well, *do* you?"

I crossed my arms and leaned my chin on my hands. "I think someone's in love with me." I sighed, smiling. "And to think, just today I was wondering what it would be like. Well, now I know . . . and it feels warm and weird all at the same time."

Lily White opened her drowsy eyes for a moment, and I stared at the distinct golden flecks in them as we sat facing each other nose to nose.

"Maybe the weird part comes from not knowing if you love someone back."

Lily White offered no help, so I went back to my sketching as she napped away our heart-to-heart talk.

"Knock, knock."

I turned to see Mom standing in the doorway. "Got a minute?"

"Sure."

She came in, leaving the door ajar. "I wondered if we could talk." I recognized the hesitation in her voice and steeled myself.

"Have a seat." I offered my bed, where the three Hebrew felines were sacked out in various states of consciousness.

"I was thinking," Mom began. "If your aunt Teri has twin girls, would you mind if I give her the baby outfits you and Faith wore?" Her deep brown eyes registered concern. Why was she asking my permission?

"It's really up to you," I replied. "I don't care either way." It was the truth. What Mom did with Faithie's and my baby things was pointless.

"Are you sure?" she probed.

I nodded. "One hundred percent, amen."

Mom smiled. "That's cute, Merry."

At first, I thought she was going to come rushing over and hug me or something, but she sat there looking like a helpless child. I swallowed the lump in my throat. No sense crying over any of this. Twins were a *doubly* special gift from God. What could I say to make Mom feel better about losing one of her own little gifts?

"What if she has boys?" I offered cheerfully.

Mom smiled. Good. That's all it took to bring her out of the doldrums. Boys . . . twin boys. Now *that* I could handle.

❧   ❧

At church that night, I ran into Jon Klein downstairs at

the water fountain. He seemed preoccupied as usual, but when I started to say something in alliteration-eze, Lissa came floating down the hall in her new springtime-blue dress, eyes shining.

"Oh, there you are," she called to him as though they'd planned to meet.

His face lit up when he saw her, and quickly I discarded the notion of speaking to him. Emotionally, I slinked back into my shell. Next to listening to Lissa's plans with Jon on the phone this afternoon, witnessing his obvious interest in her was the worst thing ever.

The two of them walked down the hall and turned to go upstairs without ever acknowledging my presence. Was I really that invisible?

I darted into the ladies' room and stared at the mirror. What incredible thing did Lissa have that I didn't? Or was it just me?

Lifting my hair up away from my face, I turned sideways. Was it my shape? I certainly wasn't as flat-chested as some girls my age. I smiled broadly at the mirror. Was it my teeth? My face? Did I smile enough?

I shrugged at the reflection in the long mirror. Wasn't Merry as merry as everyone said? Second thought—maybe Jon wanted something more than words these days. Maybe Lissa was a better choice for him, after all.

No. I had a difficult time accepting that. Bottom line: Jon had simply forgotten what we had together. The intellectual bond, the lighthearted aspect of putting words together.

I wanted to cry. The Alliteration Wizard was truly out to lunch. And out of reach.

THIRTEEN

After church, Mom made sandwiches for everyone. Skip snatched up four halves and hurried off to his room. I was surprised that he wasn't out with Nikki Klein again, but assumed he probably had tons of homework. School would be over for him in a couple weeks because he was graduating.

I took half a sandwich and wrapped it in a napkin, heading outdoors. The evening was warm and muggy from the afternoon shower. I sat under the white-latticed roof of the old gazebo in our backyard. Nibbling on my roast beef sandwich, I contemplated my sad state of affairs.

The boy I thought I was in love with liked someone else. Jon and Lissa together? Somehow their names didn't roll off my tongue the way Jon and Merry did. It was actually an effort to shape my lips to say Lissa's name after Jon's.

I whispered their names into the dim light of dusk. Over and over I spoke the words, as though saying them would help soften the blow. Soften the pain of disappointment. But the truth was, I never wanted to see them again.

I bit into my sandwich and decided it might be best to change churches. It was the only solution. But then there was another problem—school. Tomorrow!

The grass glistened in the light of a half moon, and I

pushed the back of my tennies against the gazebo step, leaning both elbows on my knees. Thinking . . . remembering.

Levi had said something that made sense today. *I am not certain about my future.* . . . He'd said it in reference to his baptism into the Amish church—a sobering thought. His hesitancy had surprised me then, but his words clicked with me now and made me aware of my own uncertainties. Especially about Jon Klein.

Why *had* Jon pursued me all through eighth grade with one word game after another? Didn't he realize that seeking a girl out like that, hanging out at her locker, having a good time with her brain, meant something?

I ate the last bite of my sandwich and stood up, brushing the crumbs off my jeans. The heavy smell of lilac hung in the air, and I breathed its perfume deep, longing for its sweetness to wash away my despair.

Sadder than sad, I walked toward the road in the shadow of a deep May moon. Planning for the future was overrated. Maybe it was better to simply live one day at a time. Maybe Levi was right. I *did* have time to decide things.

Shadrach, Meshach, and Abednego came running after me as I headed down SummerHill Lane. Lily White meowed at us, scolding because we hadn't waited for her. I retraced my steps and went back to pick her up.

"You're getting to be a demanding little so-and-so," I said, giggling into her kitty ear. When I got to the turn-off to the willow grove—the shortcut to the Zooks' farmhouse—I purposely ignored it. The light breeze felt good against my face and hair, and I slowed my walk to a stroll, enjoying the spring night.

In the distance, I heard the clip-clopping of horses and the clatter of buggy wheels heading down SummerHill.

Happy Amish teenagers wending their way to the various singings around Lancaster. The familiar sound made me think of Levi again, and I glanced toward the dirt lane leading to the Zooks'.

Levi's courting buggy was nowhere to be seen. Would he really come home alone after the singing? The fact that I'd given it another thought startled me. Where did Levi fit into my life? Or should I even be thinking about him this way? After all, the Zook family were dear friends. I didn't want to hurt them.

I snuggled Lily White next to me, then put my head down close to her, listening to the rumble of her purring. "What should I do about Levi?" I whispered. "This summer could be awfully boring with Lissa spending time with Jon."

I dreaded that thought. Not only was I losing the hope of having Jon as my boyfriend, I knew my friendship with Lissa would suffer, too.

A tiny shiver flew up my back and I pushed the painful thought out of my mind. "Maybe I *should* be Levi's girl, just for the summer," I said to my cat quartet. "What do you think?" Abednego arched his fat, black body.

I laughed out loud. "I should've known you'd be the one to protest. Come here, you!" I put Lily White down and chased after Abednego until I ran out of breath. Then, realizing it was getting late, I called the cats. Abednego didn't come at first, but what else was new.

With only three of my cats trailing behind me, I turned and headed back up the hill toward home.

❧   ❧

The next day at school, I busied myself with as many things as possible. That's what I always did when I was upset.

I tried not to notice Lissa waiting at Jon's locker. She

hadn't come in on the bus this morning. Maybe she was running late and missed it. I forced away the thought that she'd gone out after church last night. Feeling a twinge of guilt, I didn't attempt to catch her eye, or wave as usual.

I was thrilled to see Chelsea, though. She rushed down the hall toward me, calling "Merry!" as she balanced a pile of books in her arms. "You have to see these cool family crests." She opened one of the fattest books. "Check it out."

The Davis crest displayed a spear thrust through an elongated sphere with two black-and-silver dragon's wings decorating the sides.

"These *are* cool," I said. "Are you going to do yours in full color like this?"

She nodded without looking at me. "Might help my grade, don'tcha think?"

"What could go wrong with your grade?"

Chelsea glanced around for a second. "Well, you know the faith-healer aunt I was telling you about?"

"Yeah, so?"

"You don't think the teacher'll mark down for having a weirdo in the family, do you?" She snickered.

"Get a life, Chelsea." I closed my locker. "You won't get a bad grade because of an ancestor. Count on it."

She wiped her forehead and pretended to shake the perspiration off her hand. "What a relief."

"Silly you." I felt more confident about things as I passed Lissa and Jon at his locker and slipped into the bustling hallway to first period—art class.

Halfway through art, I asked Mrs. Hawkins, our expert teacher and artist-in-residence, for ideas on doing a water-color rendition of my family's crest. She suggested I do a pencil sketch on a large piece of construction paper.

"When the project is finished, you might want to mount it on tagboard," she said.

"Good idea, thanks." I went to the art supply closet and found the paints I needed but decided to wait for the tagboard till later. There was no room to store it in my locker anyway.

While I was returning to my seat, I had a peculiar idea. I could make a coat of arms for the Zooks. Even though their family name originated in Switzerland, I could create one for fun. It would be a friendly gesture, nothing more.

After supper, Uncle Pete called to fill me in on Aunt Teri's answers for the family tree. It was good of him to help me this way, and I thanked him.

"Remember to pray for your auntie," he reminded me before we said goodbye.

"Oh, we are."

"She needs all the prayers she can get."

I didn't have the courage to tell him I'd asked God for *boy* cousins. But it probably didn't matter to them. This being the first pregnancy for Aunt Teri, they would be thrilled with whatever children God gave them.

❧   ❧

All week long I was able to avoid Lissa and Jon, even though it wasn't easy. Sometimes it actually seemed as though they wanted to be isolated from the rest of us.

Chelsea noticed, too. But I was the one who brought it up. "What's with Lissa and Jon?" I asked on Friday while we waited in the cafeteria line. "They're together all the time."

"They're trying to get perfect scores on their family history projects," she said. "That's probably all it is."

I took a deep breath, clinging to my book bag for dear life.

"You're not jealous are you?" She inched closer.

"Who, me?"

Chelsea grinned. "I *know* you, Merry. You're not the martyr type."

"I need martyr's grace," I muttered, letting the first words of truth escape my lips. "But don't you dare tell a soul."

"So . . . you *do* like him!"

"Treat the truth with care," I warned her, straight-faced.

She pushed her hair away from her face, laughing. "Merry, you're such a kick. I love it when you get dramatic."

I groaned. "Let's just drop it."

"Whoa, Merry, don't take it out on me." Chelsea looked dumbfounded. "Relax, Mer. It's just a little crush, right?"

"No comment."

"It'll go away eventually. Besides, you can do better than Jon Klein." She put a carton of chocolate milk on her tray.

I glanced at the brown carton. "You'll get zits from that."

"That was an amazing leap of logic." She laughed and so did I, and together we found a table off to the side, away from the noisy meanderings of students. My mind was stuck on what she'd said about doing better than Jon. What did she mean?

Things started to settle down as we ate. We talked leisurely about our family crests and Chelsea's latest find at the library. I was even digesting my lasagna fairly well when Lissa and Jon came in together.

Instantly, my stomach lurched. I reached for my lemon-lime soda and mistakenly breathed in the sparkling spray off the top. It made me cough into my glass, nearly choking. Everyone around me stared. Jon too.

I could hardly wait for the weekend. Eighth grade had never been so traumatic!

FOURTEEN

After school, I hurried next door to see Rachel. She invited me to help with the milking. I accepted the invitation cheerfully for a change.

"*Des gut,*" she said, obviously excited.

I hurried behind her to the barn. As I helped wash down the cows for the milking, I thought of my great-great grandfather. If Joseph Lapp hadn't left the Amish way back when, I might be doing this chore twice every day.

As it turned out, I spent nearly the whole weekend with Rachel, helping her bake bread early Saturday morning. Before lunch, we weeded and watered string beans in her charity garden.

Sunday was the Lord's Day, but not a church day this week for the Zook family. The Amish attended church in one another's homes every other Sunday. On the "off" Sundays they rested, did only necessary chores, and read from their German Bibles.

As soon as I arrived home from church and ate dinner, I carefully placed the next two letters from Joseph Lapp into the wide pocket of my bib overalls. I hoped Rachel and I might have a private moment together so she could translate them for me.

When I arrived next door, Rachel was getting ready for a walk and was delighted that I had come. Together, we headed for the woods behind the barn.

"Simple things are best," I said as we walked into the deepest part of the woods together.

She understood fully, and lifted her rosy cheeks to the sun as its warm rays filtered down through the branches overhead.

"Would you mind reading some more of my great-great grandfather's letters?" I asked later while we stopped to catch our breath.

"Did ya bring 'em?"

"They're right here." I took them out of my pocket, plastic and all. We sat on the ground with the forest animals, squirrels and birds, skittering around us.

Rachel began to translate. " 'My dear Samuel, brother and friend. I have thought to change my name, my given Christian name. I wish not to bring sadness and shame to my family. I will not legally change my surname, but I have chosen to be called Levi Lapp. You will address me as Levi from this day forward.' "

"Levi?" I asked, still confused. "Why a biblical name if he was leaving the Amish?"

Rachel scanned the next lines. "It says here that Mary Smith picked out the name for him. Maybe she was a Mennonite."

"That's strange," I said.

She hung her head sadly. "I had almost forgotten about his changing names."

"Maybe he needed a clean slate to start over."

"Maybe so."

We talked about other possible reasons, but the discussion eventually led to Levi, her brother.

"Grossdawdy wants Levi to be baptized this summer right after his seventeenth birthday," she said.

I wondered about that. Did her elderly grandfather feel he could die in peace if Levi was safely baptized into the church?

"Grossdawdy is afeared for Levi," she went on, looking into my eyes. "He suspicions that Levi is running with a rough crowd. Maybe even the Mule Skinners."

I didn't dare tell her that what she said was true.

"Such things could give Grossdawdy heart failure," she said softly. "Me too."

Was she worried that history might repeat itself? That her own brother, Levi Zook, might become as rebellious as Joseph Lapp from so long ago?

We stood up and began walking again. Then, coming to a patch of wild clover, we bent low and filled our pockets. I thought of Joseph changing his name to Levi for Mary, his bride-to-be. It seemed strange that their names matched Levi's and mine. So very strange . . .

❧ ❧

Monday after school, Rachel showed me how to make a cross-stitch design without a pattern. On Tuesday, we worked on quilted pillow coverings for her hope chest. And mine.

Rachel didn't know that I owned no such thing as a hope chest. And as I sat beside her at the kitchen table hand sewing the quilted pillows, it struck me that if I were Amish, I would be steadily filling my hope chest. Just as she was. In fact, if I were Amish, I'd probably be engaged to be married a few years from now. A startling thought.

Spending time at the Zooks' helped me escape though. I had to do something to keep my mind off Lissa and Jon. They were showing up everywhere together. At school, at church. It was unbearable.

Because stress always made me hungry, I was exactly where I needed to be. Esther Zook *always* had warm, fresh bread and homemade jellies, not to mention oodles of pies. After all, food was an Amishman's middle name!

All the time I was spending with Rachel unfortunately posed an unforeseen problem. I hadn't realized it at first, but Levi was beginning to mistake my reason for being there. He kept coming around, paying more attention to me than ever. It was one thing for him to flirt with me out in his potato field, but right under his parents' noses?

I had to admit, Levi was making me nervous. Because, friends or not, I certainly didn't want Abe and Esther Zook to think I was contributing to their son's reluctance to Amish baptism. Not now, not ever!

FIFTEEN

On Thursday after school, two days before the eighth-grade church picnic, Rachel and I moved all the furniture off her front porch—three rocking chairs and several plant tables. Both of us were sweeping, stirring up a cloud of dust, when the subject of Joseph Lapp came up.

Rachel got it started. She stopped sweeping and leaned on her broom for a moment. "I asked Grossdawdy more about Joseph Lapp."

I perked up my ears. "You did?"

"Jah." She tucked a strand of light brown hair into the bun at the back of her head. "Joseph Lapp refused to return and repent to his family and the church. He must've loved his Mary a lot to give everything up for her." She sighed. "He even lost the farmland his father had planned to give him."

I was silent. *Had Levi heard this part of the story?*

"It doesn't make sense," Rachel observed. "Why would Joseph Lapp bother kneeling for baptism if he was just gonna turn around and leave?"

"It would've been better for him in the end if he hadn't taken the baptismal vow, right?"

She nodded solemnly and slowly began to sweep again. "Baptism is sacred and permanent. If you don't take it, you never have to worry about the Meidung . . . the shunning."

"So right now you're not really in *or* out of the church."

"Jah. But most Amish teens who don't take the baptism pledge end up leaving anyway. Usually they end up Mennonites."

"Why, because Mennonites allow cars and have electricity?"

"Jah."

I swept my pile of leaves and debris under the porch railing and watched it fall to the ground. "Do you think Levi *will* be baptized this summer?"

Rachel shrugged her shoulders and her blue eyes grew sad again. "I doubt Levi will do it. I heard him tell Dat that he wants to get his hair cut."

That got my attention. I wanted to ask her if she'd told Levi about the letters from my great-great grandfather, but instead, swept another clump of dried leaves away from the house.

❧   ❧

All day Levi had been cultivating the corn field, and I wanted to see him, especially after Rachel's remark about his hair. It was hard to think of Levi with a contemporary haircut. Harder still to think of being his girl. As I headed for home that evening, I went out of my way to say hi.

Instead of stopping everything and greeting me like he usually did, Levi waved. "Hullo, Merry! Come ride with me."

"I better get going," I replied. "Mom'll have supper waiting."

He grinned, looking cuter than ever. "Come back after," he said, pushing his straw hat forward, hiding his eyes.

I snickered at the cockeyed hat and walked along the row of corn to keep up with the mules and the cultivator. "What for?"

"Ach, just come, Merry. Will ya?" He said it playfully, but there was that underlying take-charge tone indicative of the Amish male. He took his hat off and shook the dust out of his hair. "Well?"

"I might," I teased, turning to go. Why was my heart beating like this?

"Will you have your answer for me tonight?"

I turned around. This boy wasn't giving up.

What should I do?

He was grinning again. "You can come back, Merry," he urged, putting his straw hat back on. "No one'll mind."

"Your grandfather might."

He frowned suddenly.

"I know he wants you to be baptized soon."

"Every Grossdawdy wants that for his offspring."

I felt like a traitor. Rachel had confided in me and here I was spilling the beans.

"*Himmel,*" Levi said. "Rachel's been talkin' out of turn." And by my silent response I was acknowledging the truth.

He waved as I stepped gingerly between the rows of corn, heading for home. Obviously, there were no hard feelings between us for what I'd said. Levi had always been one to forgive and forget. It was the Amish way.

Scurrying over the field to SummerHill Lane, I could

hardly wait for supper. Not so much from hunger, but from mere curiosity. This was the night I would discuss Levi with my parents. I could only hope my brother wouldn't make things difficult for me. Wishful thinking. Ridiculing his "little Merry" was one of the things Skip did best.

❦   ❦

"You're right on time," Mom said as I breezed into the kitchen. "Hurry and wash up for supper."

It bothered me that she was still saying the same things she'd said to me all my life. I wasn't a kid anymore. Why didn't she realize that?

I glanced around the kitchen. Usually my brother was stuffing his face nonstop with junk food before *and* after each meal. "Where's Skip?"

Dad strolled in from the living room carrying the newspaper under his arm. "He's busy at church. The senior-high banquet's tomorrow night."

I breathed a tremendous sigh of relief. So obvious was it that Mom frowned and glanced at Dad. "Your brother will be involved in many senior activities between now and graduation day," she said. "He's excited, and I hope you're happy for him, too."

"Sure, Mom, I'm happy."

I'm happier for me, though. I headed down the hall to the powder room to wash up. Come next fall, I'd have the run of the house.

"I always knew that boy had it in him," Dad remarked as I came back into the kitchen. "Skip sure had us fooled in middle school, though."

Mom said, "High school seemed to make the big difference for him. I guess change is good sometimes."

Her comment reminded me of Jon Klein. That's exactly what I'd said to him—*change is good*—the day I worried out loud about going to high school next year. It was also the last day we'd played our alliteration word game together. Thirteen depressing days ago!

Dad refolded the newspaper and slid it into a large wicker basket under Mom's square antique plant table in the corner of the kitchen. She had succeeded in coaxing a multitude of African violets to life in that corner; now they were thriving to beat the band.

Dad offered to carry the platter of fried chicken to the table and sat down, waiting as Mom filled our glasses with iced tea. He looked at me from the head of the table. "You're awfully quiet, Mer. Something on your mind?"

I wondered whether to spring Levi Zook on them now or later. Opting for later, I reached for my napkin and shrugged. "We can talk about it during dessert."

"Which reminds me," Mom said, observing me. "I made chocolate chip cookies this morning."

I sniffed the air. "Can't wait. Smells great!"

Mom smiled and bowed her head.

Dad said a prayer of thanks for the food, and I ate while the two of them chatted about his day at the hospital. Evidently, a woman in labor had come to the emergency room. "She looked large enough for twins," Dad said, grinning at me, "but it turned out she gave birth to one very hefty baby boy."

"I wonder how everything's going with Aunt Teri," Mom said. "Haven't talked to her for over a week."

"She's certainly no spring chicken," Dad said, chuckling. "You have to hand it to her, wanting to start a family at her age."

I could hardly wait for the chocolate chip cookies. My parents were simply rambling, enjoying their conversation about absolutely nothing while I sat here stewing, thinking through my plan of attack.

Mom started to clear the table, and I hopped up to help. Anything to get things rolling.

At last, the ice cream was dished up and the heaping plate of cookies placed on the table. Dad smiled almost sweetly at me, leaned back in his chair, and waited. Waited silently with his arms folded across his chest.

The silence wiped me out, and I took a deep breath, hoping I could pull this off. "Mom, Dad"—I looked at both of them—"what would you say if I went out with Levi Zook?"

Silence followed. Absolute, complete silence.

Hilarious laughter would've been welcomed at this point. Anything.

But Dad's face was as blank as Mom's.

SIXTEEN

"Well?" I ventured, still waiting for some kind of response from them. "Levi *is* a good friend, and we've known each other since childhood."

Dad took another cookie, held it in midair, and turned it around in his hand as if it were a buggy wheel. "So it *was* you in Levi's buggy two Sundays ago."

I gasped. "What?"

His face broke into a broad grin. "Miss Spindler just happened to mention it to me the other day when I was mowing the lawn."

"I should've known," I muttered.

"Don't be upset, Mer," Dad said, surprising me. "You know how the old lady is. She makes mountains out of molehills."

I nodded. "It's her livelihood."

Mom hadn't commented on the matter yet, and her aloofness made me nervous.

Dad continued. "Where do you plan to go with Levi?"

"He talked about the Green Dragon." I shrugged my shoulders.

Mom spoke at last. "I hope you won't go out on the

highway in that buggy of his." She stared at me, her eyes penetrating. Then, she cut loose with her real concern. "Merry . . . what could you possibly have in common with an Amish boy?"

Now *I* was the one leaning back in my chair. I needed space all of a sudden, and Mom wasn't helping things by inching her face closer and closer to mine. Her eyes burned into me, and I resented her attitude. I slid my chair away from the table.

"Merry, I—"

Dad interrupted her. "Look, I don't see any harm in Merry spending some time with her friend. Levi's a great kid. Good manners, as far as I can tell."

Mom argued. "But Merry's only thirteen." I was wondering when she'd pull out that excuse.

Dad reached for her hand. "Darling, our daughter will be fourteen soon. It's not like she's going out with some stranger. The two of them have literally grown up together. Besides, Levi's family, in a very distant way."

That wasn't good enough for Mom. "But he's lots older than Merry. Next thing, he'll be looking for a wife."

Dad nodded, sneaking a wink at me. "You're absolutely right. You've gotta watch those Amish boys. They ride around in those noisy courting buggies all hours of the night, snatching up pretty young things, going off to the bishop, and getting married."

I stood up. "Marriage is the last thing on my mind!"

Mom smiled sympathetically. "You have many more years ahead of you to decide such important things."

"So . . . you don't mind then?" I asked, looking first at Dad, then at Mom.

With true reluctance, Mom managed to utter, "I guess one time won't hurt."

"Promise not to tell Skip?" I said. "That is *if* I decide to go."

Dad put his fingers together like a boy scout. "I promise." He was such a tease sometimes.

I loaded the dishwasher for Mom, insisting that she relax with Dad in the living room. The Levi discussion was behind me!

Now there was only one thing left to do.

Suddenly unsure of myself, I pictured Levi working the corn field with his mule team and cultivator, loosening the soil. Waiting for my answer.

When the kitchen was spotless, I headed outside to the gazebo. I sat on the railing, dangling my legs over the edge, facing the willow grove. I stared at the dense, graceful trees that blocked my view of Zooks' farm. The willows were like a barrier between the Amish world and my own.

I closed my eyes and imagined what life would've been like if Faithie, my twin, were still alive. She would be sitting here on the railing beside me, encouraging me not to shut Mom out the way I had . . . to hang on to my feelings for Jon Klein even though he'd hurt me. She would tell me to pray about going out with Levi. And she would hug me and tell me I was her best friend.

Best friend. How I missed her!

A half hour later, the back door opened and Dad called to me, "Merry, someone's on the phone for you."

I leaped off the gazebo and ran into the house to the kitchen. "Hello?"

"Hi, Mer. It's Chelsea."

"What's up?"

"Just thought I'd check something out." She paused. "Look, I can't believe this could be true, knowing you, Mer, but my mom ran into your nosy neighbor at the post office today."

Gulp!

"Old Hawk Eyes said you and Levi were out riding in his courting buggy."

I laughed. "That lady gets around." Then I explained about the thunderstorm. "It was just a neighborly gesture. Really."

"C'mon, Merry," she persisted. "You were always so . . . so, uh . . . attracted to the guy."

"Attracted?"

"You know how you always watch him when we ride past his house on the school bus."

"But it's not what you think—I mean, I'm not ready to join the Amish or anything."

"You're sure?"

I took a deep breath. To tell the truth, I *had* been toying with the thought. "Look, Chelsea," I said. "If I tell you something, will you promise not to tell a single soul?"

"*Now* what?"

"Levi asked me to be his girlfriend."

She gasped. Literally gasped and kept doing it. Finally, when she caught her breath, she said, "Are you kidding?"

I felt an overwhelming sense of confidence. Even more so than when I'd shared the news with my parents.

"What did you tell him?" She sounded dramatically serious. The way I usually sounded under similar circumstances.

"I haven't told him anything yet," I replied. "I was just on my way over there."

"Oh, Merry, please don't do anything stupid."

"Stupid?"

"Merry, don't be weird about this. Please." She sounded desperate.

"You've never met Levi Zook, have you?"

"What's that got to do with anything?"

"Absolutely everything! You have no idea what you're saying, so if you don't mind, I think we better end this conversation now before—"

"Merry, listen to me!"

I clammed up. She was making me mad.

Her voice grew softer. "Don't do anything, Mer. Okay? I'll be right over."

"Don't you dare!" Now I was furious. "And don't treat me like a kid," I blurted. "I'm old enough to decide things like this. Besides, you said I could do better than Jon, remember?"

She exhaled into the phone. "Why do you take everything so literally? I didn't mean you should go off and *marry* some Amish guy."

"Excuse me? Who said anything about that?"

"But have you thought this through? Have you considered the consequences?" she asked.

If I hadn't known better, I would've thought she'd been playing Jon's alliteration game!

"Trust me, Chelsea. Levi's just a good friend," I said.

"Well, you can bet on this, I'm going to do whatever it takes to bring you to your senses!"

And with that, she hung up. Before I could even say goodbye.

SEVENTEEN

Levi was long gone from the corn field when I finally wandered over to the Zook farm. From his side of the willow grove, I could see the gas lamp burning in the kitchen and assumed they were having supper. Amish farmers worked outdoors as long as there was light, then ate a hearty meal as dusk approached.

Lily White's soft little head and paws hung out over the top of my bib overalls. The wide chest pocket was one of her favorite places, and she purred loudly as she rode there—next to my heart.

I strolled past the new white barn and out to the pond and the spacious meadow where the willow grove ended. Wide and very deep, the pond stretched across a large area, embracing both the Zooks' property and ours.

Sitting down on the cool grass, I freed Lily White, letting her roam as she pleased. It was almost nighttime, but it wasn't dark. The sky was filled with tiny lights as if someone had flicked a paintbrush across the universe. And the longer I sat there, the brighter the dots of lights became.

I found the broad, luminous band of the Milky Way and

the moon—a fat fingernail sliver. Its light cast a splendid ribbon across the pond.

Relaxing there in the grass just yards from the placid water, I began to pray as I faced the sky. "Lord, you know how things are with Levi and me. I don't have to tell you that he's my friend . . . and I like him. But honestly, I don't know whether to say yes or no." I sighed. "I've never really had a boyfriend before. This is all so new to me."

I breathed in the fragrance of lilacs and continued. "Dad didn't give me such a horrible time about going out with Levi. I really thought he would. And Mom? Well, you know how moms are."

I stopped. Someone was walking toward me.

Squinting into the dim light of dusk, I recognized the long strides and the tall, lean silhouette as Levi. My heart sank. Not because I didn't want to see him, but because he'd probably ask for my answer. Again.

Quickly, I prayed some more, having a difficult time finishing. Levi could *not* be in on what I was saying about him to God. Not that it was bad or anything. Actually, it was just the opposite.

"Hi, Levi," I said as he came swishing barefoot through the grassy meadow.

"Merry." He said it softly. "I thoughtcha weren't gonna come."

"Something came up." I didn't mention Chelsea's phone call. What she'd said didn't matter anyway.

"Well, you're here now." He sat beside me, a long piece of straw hanging out of his mouth.

Lily White came over and sniffed his bare feet. I laughed and reached for her. I cradled her furry body in my arms.

"You remember Lily, don't you?"

"How can I forget?" Levi grinned at me.

Side-by-side, we listened to the sounds of night. Loud, chirping crickets. And the flutter of wings as purple martins flew home to roost in the Zooks' multileveled birdhouse.

"Remember the day you saved my life?" Levi asked unexpectedly.

"As clear as yesterday."

He laughed softly. "I was eleven and you were only eight."

"Almost nine."

He took the straw out of his mouth and tossed it on the ground. "I knew it then, Merry."

My heart pounded. *What* did he know?

Levi turned his face to the sky. "Have you ever seen a more beautiful sky?" He seemed to like asking questions that didn't require answers. I smiled, appreciating his love for God's creation. Wishing the question about being his girl could go unanswered, too.

We sat very still gazing at the twinkling lights overhead. I don't know how long we sat there, but it was long enough for the moon to climb halfway up the silo.

Suddenly, Levi stood up. "Look there!"

I saw it, too. A dazzling stream of light falling across the sky.

"Quick! Make a wish," he said, and our eyes followed the star's journey as it topped the barn and fell over the horizon.

"Come, let's walk," he said, and I pushed Lily White down inside my overalls once again. Levi laughed as I got

Lily situated. "Aren'tcha supposed to catch a falling star and put *that* in your pocket?"

I looked at him and smiled. "Lily White is as white as any star up there." Then I turned my gaze to the sky. "What a truly beautiful sight," I said, referring to the falling star. "I don't know when I've seen such a thing."

"It means something, jah?"

I knew some Amish were a little superstitious. For instance, a bride and groom wouldn't think of singing on their wedding day because they believed that singing today meant weeping tomorrow.

"What on earth could it mean?" I asked, not realizing how naive I sounded until the words were out.

Levi stopped walking. "Think of it, Merry. We sat there by the pond just now where my life nearly ended. I would've drowned that day without you." He looked up at the sky, making a sweeping motion with his hand. "And then the star falls right before our eyes. It surely must be providence, Merry. Nature's telling us something."

I almost laughed at the way he was making such a big deal of this. "You made a wish, right?"

"Did you?" he asked.

I shook my head. "I don't believe in falling stars. I'd rather pray about my dreams and wishes."

He touched my arm. "*You* can make my wish come true."

The air was filled with romance, and I thought this was how it should be. When a boy loves a girl.

"Levi Lapp loved Mary Smith," Levi was saying as we began to walk again. "Levi and Mary. Don't you see? History repeats itself."

"Are you saying that just because our ancestors had the same names?" I couldn't see the logic in this.

"Oh, it's much more than that, Merry," he said, emphatically. "It's providence."

"Well, I'm not as sure about this as you are."

"I know," he said, softly, "but maybe you will be someday."

The moon was high in the sky now. It was late, and Mom would worry. "Guess I'd better head for home."

"I'll walk ya," he offered.

"That's okay, I know the way."

I was surprised, but he let me go. And all the way home, his words echoed in my brain. *Levi and Mary.*

Levi and Merry.

EIGHTEEN

So this is how it's going to be, I thought as I stared into my locker the next morning. *Chelsea's going to snub me just because of Levi.*

She'd made things instantly clear on the bus this morning. "In case you didn't know it, Merry, you're making a major mistake if you date that Levi boy," she said flat out.

"It's none of your business." I could be just as stubborn.

Chelsea had turned away, acting offended. In fact, she ignored me the rest of the ride, but I didn't let it bother me.

Later, after English, I was rushing to change books at my locker when I noticed her talking to Jon in the hallway near the principal's office. Lissa was hovering nearby, too, obviously interested in what was being said.

It struck me as strange. Why would the three of them be hanging out together? It didn't add up. Besides that, Ashley Horton hurried over to join them as though she was expected to show up, too.

I found my social studies notebook on the top shelf of my locker. It was bursting with information for the Hanson family history. Quickly, I deposited my English books and without another glance at the foursome, slammed my locker door and hurried off to class.

Just before the bell rang, the four of them rushed into class, and when I caught Chelsea's eye she looked rather sheepish. I pretended not to notice and gathered my outline and family reports as I waited for the teacher to begin.

"All family histories are due on Tuesday," she said, reminding us that this Monday was Memorial Day. As if we needed reminding! "Please be prepared to give an oral report as well."

No problem. My work was basically done. All I had left to do was enter my data on Dad's computer over the weekend and print it out.

During the last half of class, we were allowed to work together with our partners. I motioned for Chelsea to come to my side of the room so we could confer on things. Reluctantly, she came.

"Are you done with your interviews?" I asked as she sat in the desk across the aisle from me.

"All but two." She leaned over to look at my sketch. "Hey, what a cool coat of arms."

"Oh, that," I said, pushing the sketch behind some other papers. "It's the family crest for a friend of mine." I didn't tell her it was a gift for the Zooks.

"So where's yours?" she asked.

I shuffled through my papers. "Here." I held it up. "I plan on blowing it up and putting it on tagboard in full color. What do you think?"

She took the sketch and studied it for a moment. "This is really good. You could be a commercial artist someday."

"It's not *that* good, but thanks."

She found her family interviews and had me proofread them for spelling errors. Grammar, too. I liked the format she'd used to set up the questions and answers on her computer.

"This looks really professional," I told her.

She slumped down in her chair. "If only I didn't have to mention my great-aunt Essie."

"Lots of kids would probably like to have someone as colorful and fascinating in their family tree."

She pushed her hair back from her face. "What? Like Amish *traitors*?"

I didn't like the way she emphasized traitors as though I might be one myself. "My great-great grandfather made a choice for love," I explained in a whisper. "It wasn't easy for him to leave the Amish."

She nodded her head, patronizing me. "Right. And what about you and Levi? Did you see him last night?"

I nodded, egging her on. "It was enchanting, really. You should've seen the stars."

"Spare me the dramatics."

I felt frustrated. "Nothing you can say or do will make a difference. It's my choice."

"Well," she said slyly, "I guess we'll just have to see about that."

I had no idea what she meant, and to tell the truth, I really didn't care.

❧   ❧

Mom was waiting for me on the front porch as I came up the side yard. "Merry," she called. "You have new baby cousins. Uncle Pete just called from the hospital."

I hurried up to the white columned porch and sat on the step. "The babies must've come early," I said, hesitating to ask about the sex of the twins.

"They're four weeks premature," Mom said. "Not too bad for a first pregnancy, especially twins."

"Are the babies healthy?"

She nodded, smiling. "Benjamin and Rebekah are doing just fine. So well, in fact, they'll be released from the hospital tomorrow."

"A boy and a girl?" This was truly amazing.

"One of each," she said. "And the proud parents couldn't be happier."

"So . . . whose clothes are you gonna send them? Mine or Faithie's?"

She leaned forward suddenly. "Which do you prefer, Merry?"

I thought we'd already had this conversation. "It really doesn't matter, Mom. Do what you want." She'd never dressed us alike as babies. The look-alike thing came later in grade school, and then only on special occasions like birthdays and Easter.

I could see it was going to be a tough decision for Mom, choosing whose baby things—Faithie's or mine—to give away. She had that distant look in her eyes again, and it made me wonder if she would ever get over Faithie's death.

"I'm starved," I said, getting up and going inside.

Mom followed and insisted on peeling an apple for me. I sat at the kitchen table as she washed her hands, then reached for a paring knife from the wooden knife rack. Why did it always seem as though she needed to talk things out, but couldn't? Every time we got the slightest bit close to whatever was bugging her, she'd clam up. It reminded me of Chelsea and the way she shut me out the minute I mentioned God or the Bible.

I ended up eating my apple quarters alone in the kitchen. Well, alone if you didn't count the cats. I guess they just assumed that if someone was snacking, they should be, too.

Mom excused herself to go upstairs, and I figured it probably had something to do with choosing baby clothes for little Rebekah. Knowing the way Mom usually avoided the attic, I decided to stay out of her way. There was absolutely nothing I could do to help her now. Not unless she opened up and stopped playing these games. Nearly seven years had passed since Faithie's death. Why couldn't Mom talk with me about it?

In between bites of apple, I recited the babies' nicknames out loud. "Benny and Becky." Cute names, I thought. Alliterated, too.

And for the first time in two weeks, I didn't feel wiped out about the Alliteration Wizard and his recent alliance with Lissa.

NINETEEN

I nearly swallowed my tonsils when Jon Klein called later that evening. "Mistress Merry," he said when I answered the phone.

"Jon?"

"A bunch of us are going to help serve at the senior banquet tonight at church. Want to come?"

"Oh . . . I didn't know," I said, floundering for the right words.

"Well, I thought you might want to help."

"Uh . . . thanks."

I thought the conversation was over when he said, "Oh, Merry, what about the picnic tomorrow? You'll be there, won't you?"

"Haven't decided yet." And after I said that, I wished I hadn't. Now he knew I didn't have a date.

"You really oughta come, Mer, since we're all graduating from eighth grade together." It was very thoughtful of him to call. But why now?

All of us kids from church, and several others like Chelsea Davis, had gone through most of grade school and all of middle school together. Except Lissa. She'd moved here toward the end of seventh grade.

"So, what do you say?" he asked again.

"I'm, uh . . . I might be busy."

For a long, unbearable moment he didn't say anything. Then, at last, "Well, I hope to see you."

We both said goodbye, and I held on to the receiver as I placed it in its cradle as though it were my only link to him.

That's when I remembered we hadn't played the alliteration game just now. And I felt a twinge of sadness.

After supper, Dad decided he wanted some soft ice cream. So the three of us hopped into the car and headed for the Dairy Queen. Since Skip was busy with Nikki Klein and his graduation banquet, it was nice to get out with Mom and Dad by myself.

When we drove past our church, I thought about Jon's invitation. There had been that same friendly ring to his voice. But I wondered why he'd called, really. Especially since he and Lissa were together.

Mom started discussing the new babies, and I eased back into the soft padding of the booth, waiting for our ice cream orders. Dad came up with the bright idea for Mom to go to New Jersey and help Aunt Teri with the twins.

"Why don't you go tomorrow?" he suggested.

Mom protested a bit. "But it's Memorial Day weekend."

Dad glanced at me. "We can manage for a few days. Can't we, Mer?"

I nodded my consent. "Besides, it'll be fun for you to help with the babies." I caught myself before saying that it would be like old times. Even so, I couldn't help but think it would be good for Mom to be around newborn twins again.

Dad put his arm around Mom. "What do you think, hon?"

"Well, I know Teri will need an extra pair of hands."

"Then it's settled," Dad said just as his hot fudge sundae came.

Mom's eyebrows shot up when she saw her banana split. "Are you sure you're not trying to get rid of me?"

"Oh, Mom, really." I picked up a spoon and dipped into the rich, creamy goo on top of my peanut butter sundae.

She studied me for a moment. "You won't be going off and marrying Levi Zook while I'm gone, will you?"

"Right," I said. "It's not like you don't have to notify the Amish bishop ahead of time and everything. Besides, the Amish around here get married in November."

Dad grinned at Mom. "Sounds as though she's thought this through, wouldn't you say?"

"Dad!"

Mom frowned, looking far too serious. "Merry, promise me you won't go riding in his buggy again."

"Levi and I aren't going out in his buggy," I assured her. I could've saved her a lot of concern by telling her I hadn't agreed to go *anywhere* with him.

❧   ❧

Saturday dawned long before I chose to crawl out of bed. Mom had other plans for me. She had an agenda, all right, and barged into my room to inform me of it. "You'll be the only female around here while I'm gone," she stated.

"Female?" I mumbled from under my comforter. *What was that supposed to mean?*

"You know what I'm talking about."

I was still sleepy eyed from the sandman, and here she was rehearsing Dad's hospital schedule and telling me when Skip was supposed to be home.

"Can't you write it down?" I said. "What time is it anyway?"

"I've been up for hours packing and arranging meals and things, Merry. The least you can do is cooperate for one minute."

"What?" I sat up.

"You heard me." She got up and flung my bathrobe at the bed, covering my cats. They didn't seem to mind the terry cloth feel of my robe next to them. In fact, they began rearranging themselves on it, which only infuriated Mom. "Honestly, you have way too many cats."

This was the first I'd heard such a thing.

"We really need to talk about this problem." She glared at my beloved babies.

"How can you say that?" I replied, now fully awake. "They're not a problem to me, or anyone else." *Except for Skip,* I thought disgustedly.

"I should've said something long ago," came her terse response.

"But, Mom."

"I really don't have time for this now," she said, standing at the foot of my bed in her traveling clothes—a yellow sweat suit and tennies to match. Her graying hair was pulled back into a clump at the back of her neck and fastened with a bright yellow organdy tie bow. Honestly, she looked like a canary.

She glanced at her watch. "It's already seven o'clock," she said. "Can you be downstairs in five minutes?"

I groaned, falling back onto my pillow. "How could you do this to me?"

She didn't respond with words but turned on her heels and left the room. I could hear her doing the same thing to Skip down the hall, waking him up too early.

What was bothering her? Was it the fact that her younger sister had given birth to twins?

I hated to disturb my cats, but I needed my robe. If I didn't show up in a flash, Mom would really be upset.

Wandering into my bathroom, I stretched. *Mom isn't herself these days*, I thought, reaching for a washcloth. She irritated me, yet I felt sorry for her. Faithie, her daughter, was dead—nothing could ever change that. But what bothered me even more was the fact that *I* was alive—and being treated like this.

I knew better than to dawdle when Mom had deadlines, so I hustled downstairs. She was already writing things in her lined tablet. "There's a salmon casserole dish in the refrigerator for supper tonight," she began. "Just warm it up in the microwave for the three of you."

"That's easy," I said, noticing the suitcase beside the back door. And a duffle bag bursting with baby clothes, no doubt.

She continued to rattle on about additional dinner possibilities, when to do laundry, and would I please pick up the house for the cleaning lady? "You won't forget anything, will you?"

"The list is all I need."

She pushed it across the table. "Better put it on the refrigerator or somewhere safe."

"Relax, Mom, everything'll be fine."

"Well, I hope so." She stood up then. "I'm counting on you, Merry."

That's when I noticed how vulnerable and sad she looked. I moved toward her, wanting to hug her. "You can always count on me, Mom. You know that."

Tears sprang to her eyes, and she darted toward the table. Away from me.

Sadly, I watched her pick up the list and put it on the refrigerator, turning her back on me. Strange as it seemed, posting her list on the fridge was somehow more important than my hug.

TWENTY

Getting up early on a Saturday wasn't so bad, really. It meant that I could spend more time at the Zooks'.

Before I left, I finished making their family crest, outlining the watercolored sections with black marker. Then, carefully, I rolled it up, carrying it under my arm.

Mom left in a hurry once we discussed her list, and as far as I could tell, Skip had gone back to bed. Dad would be tied up at the hospital till six tonight. Basically, I had the day to myself.

Esther Zook was delighted with my present, and promptly hung the colorful drawing on the kitchen wall. I was surprised because the Amish usually didn't decorate their walls much.

"This is so kind of you, Merry," Esther said, standing back to admire it.

"I'm glad you like it," I said.

Rachel began to set the table. "Will you stay and eat the noon meal with us?"

I remembered my promise to Mom this morning. She

131

was counting on me to make sure things ran smoothly at home. "Better not today," I said, explaining that Skip was probably just getting up and would be starved.

"Come back later, jah?"

"After lunch."

Levi seemed pleased that I was spending the day there, and later, when he and I went to the barn to round up the cows for milking, he asked, "Why didja make us the drawing?"

"I wanted to." I pulled on a pair of old rubber work boots belonging to Levi's father.

He studied me hard. "You put a five-pointed star right in the middle," he said. "Does that mean something?"

"I just made it up," I explained. "There are no real family crests for the name *Zook*. And the star just seemed to fit." I chuckled, remembering the falling star that night by the pond.

"I don't think you can laugh when providence comes knocking." His eyes were serious.

"Well . . . maybe."

"Not *maybe*, Merry," he said. "Providence is something we Amish folk live by."

It was interesting to hear him say "we Amish."

"I thought you weren't sure about your future here on the farm." My words were sincere, and I saw by his face that he hadn't misunderstood.

"Providence must be attended to no matter what," he went on. "Just think what might've happened if your great-great grandfather had not married outside the Amish."

"What? You think *that* was providential?"

"You, Merry, would not be here today if Levi Lapp had

not married Mary Smith." He turned to me, his face soft and quizzical. "That's providence. A very gut thing!"

The sweet smell of hay made the moment stand out in my mind long afterward.

❧   ❧

Rachel and her sisters showed up for milking right on time; little Susie, too. They stared at my giant boots, caked with dried cow manure, and giggled.

"Sorry"—I glanced at their muddy bare feet—"but I'm not quite ready for squishy stuff between my toes." While we washed down the cows for milking, I enjoyed the chatter around me. Rachel and Ella Mae, Nancy and little Susie, engaging in the art of conversation. Pennsylvania Dutch style.

I felt at home here. True, these girls—Levi, too—were distant cousins, but deep in my heart I knew they might be much more. Maybe even my destiny.

After milking and helping Rachel tend her charity garden, I headed home. Minus the work boots, naturally. I thought of Levi's words. *You, Merry, would not be here today...*

I wasn't exactly sure how I felt about all this talk of providence, but I did know one thing: history didn't have to repeat itself unless the people involved allowed it. Levi Lapp and Mary Smith really and truly had nothing to do with how Levi Zook and Merry Hanson lived out their lives.

Skipping through the willows, I felt good, surprising myself that not once had I thought about the eighth-grade picnic. Or Jon Klein.

The thoughts came later, though—after supper when

Chelsea called. "Hey, you'll never guess what," she said. "I went to church today."

"To the picnic?" I was thrilled; this was a good first step for an atheist. "How was it?"

"Okay, I guess, for a *church* picnic."

I overlooked her remark.

"You should've come, Mer," she said, a question in her voice. "Everyone was asking about you. I even heard that Jon called you from the church office."

"He did?"

Twice in two days!

"You mean you didn't talk to him?"

"I was gone all day," I admitted. Then I asked, "Did Lissa know Jon called?"

"How should *I* know?" She sounded vague. "You know how these boy/girl things are."

I wanted a straight answer. "Did Jon hang out with Lissa or not?"

"Why don't you find out straight from the horse's mouth?"

"Why should I call him when *you* were there?"

"Oh, Merry, you're being a stubborn mule."

"Thanks a lot."

Neither of us spoke for a moment. Then she said, "You said you were gone. Does that mean you were with Levi?"

I couldn't tell her about my long day at the Zook farm. I just couldn't. To tell an outsider about the way I'd interacted with my Amish friends would take away some of the specialness.

Instead, I shared the news about Aunt Teri's babies, which instantly got her off the Levi subject.

"Aw, you're kidding, you have twin cousins?"

"Uh-huh, and I think my aunt and uncle are coming up next month. Maybe you can see the babies then."

"What did they name them?"

"Benjamin and Rebekah."

"How sweet. Benny and Becky."

I laughed. "I thought of that, too. But I'm not so sure my aunt's gonna want nicknames just yet."

"Why not?" She was actually in a great mood now, and I was relieved.

"Oh, you know how new mothers are," I said. "They want their offspring to start out with good, solid names. That's why my parents named me Merry, for one thing. They never dreamed I'd get pegged with a nickname."

She laughed. "And so you get Mer all the time."

"Yeah." I thought of my twin sister. "And Faith got Faithie."

"I remember," she said softly.

After we said goodbye, I set the table and warmed up the casserole dish Mom had made early this morning. Skip didn't have much to say other than that Jon had called. Old news.

Dad looked worn out from a hectic day in the emergency room. As soon as we finished with supper, I heard him shuffle down the hall to his study—probably to call Mom long distance.

I didn't feel like a fight, so I didn't bother asking Skip for help cleaning up the kitchen. The minute things were spotless, I hurried upstairs to the attic.

I had told Mom it didn't matter which baby clothes she took along for baby Rebekah. And I truly felt that it didn't matter. But after my conversation with Mom this morning—and the indifferent way she had treated me, getting me up early and forcing me to listen to her instructions while I was half asleep—I wanted to know whether she'd taken Faithie's clothes or mine.

I groped around for the attic light switch, encouraging Lily White to curl up somewhere. Wanting to be near me always, my little "shadow" had followed me up the steep steps.

Quickly, I located the boxes marked baby clothes. Several sat open and empty on the floor. My heart pounded as I opened first one, and then the other, of the remaining boxes. I knew it was probably ridiculous to feel this way, but I had decided while cleaning up the kitchen that if Mom had given Faithie's baby things away, it was a good sign. A sign that she was beginning to deal with her loss. A sign that I was as dear to her as the memory of her other daughter.

Lily White couldn't stay away from the action and rubbed her head against my arm. Her softness comforted me as I knelt on the thick carpet and peered into the first box. I braced myself for the worst.

TWENTY-ONE

Mom had always dressed me in baby blues and soft yellows. Faithie had worn greens and pinks.

Tears stung my eyes as I picked frilly *blue* dresses and lacy *yellow* playsuits out of the box. I held my tiny outfits near my heart, sobbing.

Lily White sensed my emotion and jumped into my lap, purring away like a mini-motor. In the quiet of the somewhat musty attic room, I laughed and cried for joy.

On Tuesday, Chelsea and I presented our family history reports to the class. She held up my family crest while I pointed to the lion, representing my courageous ancestry. When I told about Levi Lapp and Mary Smith, I noticed Jon Klein lean forward, paying close attention. Had he caught the similarity of names?

Chelsea was next. I held up her family tree while she went through her generations on both sides. No one even cracked a smile when she told about her great-aunt Essie Peterson, the faith healer. I knew all along it would be just fine.

After class, I was gathering up my books when Jon came over to my desk. "We missed you at the picnic Saturday," he said.

Who was *we?*

"Sounds like it was great." I hadn't thought I'd missed anything by not going. But maybe I had, and by the way Jon was grinning from ear to ear, it looked as though he was mighty glad we were having this talk.

Only a few kids were left in the room, including Chelsea. When she saw us together, she exited quickly. And there was Lissa, but she was busy talking to the teacher.

"Did your brother tell you I called?" Jon asked.

"Uh-huh." I was dying to ask why he'd called, but didn't.

"I haven't seen you around much," he said.

I picked up my books. "You know how it is with big projects this time of year."

He looked concerned. As if there was something else on his mind. As if he didn't believe what I'd just said.

Then Lissa came over. "Hi, Merry. Long time no see." Like that was *my* problem. She handed Jon some papers. "Well, see you two," she said and left.

What was going on?

"Well, the bus'll be here any minute," I said. "I'd better get going."

Jon followed me to my locker. "Say that with all *b*'s," he said.

I grinned a bit too broadly and reached for my combination lock. Jon leaned over, looking at me comically. "So . . . does this smile say something?"

Opening my locker, I said, "Say that with all *s*'s!"

"I just did!"

The guy was good. I'd forgotten how good.

"Wait right here, Merry." He rushed off to his locker, threw his books inside, and slammed the door. What was on his mind? And where was Lissa?

"We have to talk," he said, following me out to the bus.

"What's up?" I thought this might be about Lissa. Maybe he needed some womanly advice.

On the bus, once the noise rose to a dull roar, he started talking. "Merry, I hope you won't take this wrong, but some of us were talking, and . . ." He paused as though he wasn't sure what to say.

"About what?"

He took a deep breath. "It's just my opinion, but I think you're missing out on a lot."

I was confused. "What are you saying?"

He looked miserable. Absolutely miserable. As though he wished he hadn't started this. "Hanging out with that Amish guy keeps you from—"

"Excuse me?" I shouted.

Jon waved his hands. "No, no! Relax, don't get on Chelsea's case. Please! She's just concerned. All of us are."

I felt my face scrunching up. "Look, I don't interfere in *your* life, what right do you have—"

"Don't be ticked, Merry. It's just a friendly suggestion." He actually looked sincere. He sighed. "None of us think you belong with the Amish."

I turned around to look for a vacant seat toward the back. Anywhere on earth would be better than sitting next to Jon Klein. Anywhere!

Spotting Lissa, I motioned for her to trade seats with

me. "Thanks for nothing," I said to Jon. Then, sliding out of my seat, I made my way back to where Lissa had been sitting next to Chelsea.

She was wearing a mischievous grin. "*Someone* had to bring you back to your senses," Chelsea said, her green eyes flashing. "I knew Jon was the best choice."

"Well, it didn't work."

A question mark in the shape of a frown slid between her eyes. "What are you thinking, Mer?"

I refused to respond.

"Okay, go ahead and be Amish," she taunted. "Have a nice life, but don't say I didn't warn you."

The bus took an eternity to get to SummerHill, but when it stopped at the willow grove, I leaped out of my seat and dashed down the aisle.

Outside, I stood in the road, watching the bus chug-a-lug up the hill. "Good riddance," I said, as much to the sputtering, coughing school bus as to my former friends. Maybe now I knew firsthand, on a small scale, what it was like to be shunned.

I began running up the hill to my house. Hard. But something was changing in me. I was beginning to feel tall now. Tall and proud. Jon couldn't hurt me like this. I wouldn't let him. I'd . . .

It was then that I knew I didn't need to run. I could do anything I wanted to. Jon Klein or not. My life didn't revolve around the Alliteration Wizard!

❧   ❧

Several days passed before I saw Levi again. He was hitching Apple up to the family buggy in front of the house when I walked down their lane.

"Hi, Merry." He tipped his straw hat, keeping it high off his head for a moment.

I stared at his hair. Short!

"You got a haircut?" I said.

He removed his hat completely, proudly displaying his shingled hair. "Do ya like it?"

"It's . . . it's not very Amish," I said.

"You're not sore about it, are ya, Merry?"

"Just surprised." I couldn't get over how modern he looked. Except for his white shirt, black trousers, and the tan suspenders he always wore.

He finished hitching up the horse, and before his mother and little Susie came down the steps, he put his hat back on. "Let's take a walk, jah?"

"Okay." I had a feeling it was close to being the right time to give him my answer. A long-awaited one.

We walked through the side yard and back around to the barn. Then up the earthen ramp to the second level and the hayloft.

I grinned as Levi opened the double doors. He knew I loved this place. Some kids grow up playing make-believe in tree houses. We'd grown up here.

My heart did a little dance as we entered the secret world. Levi reached for the long rope and jumped on, swinging out and over the wide opening below us where the livestock were fed and stabled and where the cows were milked twice a day.

I leaned back against a bale of hay, breathing in its sweet aroma, watching him swing back and forth. This was heaven on earth!

"You want to be my girl, jah?" he said, as he flew back toward the haymow on the rope. Levi's eyes caught mine, and I was thankful he'd chosen to communicate this way. Discussing your summer while swinging on a rope probably made it easier for him, too.

There was only one word I knew Levi longed to hear. And I said it with confidence, with the best Pennsylvania Dutch accent I could muster. "Jah."

Levi leaped off the rope and hurried over to me. He held out his hand. It felt warm from the rope.

We ran down the ramp, around the barn, and through the meadow. Together.

❦   ❦

On June 3, my brainy brother graduated from high school. Nikki Klein joined us for the celebration. As much as I'd wanted to get away from Jon, if things kept going the way they were with my brother and Jon's sister, maybe he and I'd be closer than we think! Yee-ikes!

But . . . college often changes things. At least, that's what Mom said when we talked the other day. "You won't be losing your brother to another girl. At least not for a long time."

That's when she told me Skip had decided to walk in Dad's footsteps and become a medical doctor.

As for Jon, I couldn't stop thinking about how he'd stuck his neck out and talked straight to me on the bus. For a quiet guy, it probably took a lot of courage. And being a Hanson, I could definitely relate to that.

Chelsea stopped freaking out about Levi soon after school was dismissed for the summer. She told me yesterday

I could do whatever I wanted, even though she thought I'd truly flipped.

Lissa still seemed starry-eyed over Jon. Thank goodness, Chelsea never told her how I'd felt about him!

Last evening, Levi and I walked around our pond without Lily White tagging along. I didn't even think of teaching him the alliteration game; we had other things to talk about. Like how hard would it be for me to become Amish. Not for the purpose of marrying Levi someday, but just if I *wanted* to be Amish . . . for myself. For myself and my family heritage—to get my family roots back on track. To "redeem" my great-great grandfather Lapp, who went to his grave a shunned man.

It was all just talk, of course. And we didn't witness any falling stars, but *this* time, I let Levi walk me up SummerHill and back to my house.

Never once did we look into each other's faces, but a billion stars above us witnessed Levi's new haircut. And my enormous grin.

It was going to be a truly special summer.

FROM BEVERLY ... TO YOU

❧   ❧

I'm delighted that you're reading SUMMERHILL SECRETS. Merry Hanson is such a fascinating character—I can't begin to count the times I laughed while writing her humorous scenes. And I must admit, I always cry with her.

Not so long ago, I was Merry's age, growing up in Lancaster County, the home of the Pennsylvania Dutch—my birthplace. My grandma Buchwalter was Mennonite, as were many of my mother's aunts, uncles, and cousins. Some of my school friends were also Mennonite, so my interest and appreciation for the "plain" folk began early.

It is they, the Mennonite and Amish people—farmers, carpenters, blacksmiths, shopkeepers, quiltmakers, teachers, schoolchildren, and bed and breakfast owners—who best assisted me with the research for this series. Even though I have kept their identity private, I am thankful for these wonderfully honest and helpful friends.

If you want to learn more about Rachel Zook and her people, ask for my Amish bibliography when you write. I'll send you the book list along with my latest newsletter. Please include a *self-addressed, stamped envelope* for all correspondence. Thanks!

Beverly Lewis
℅ Bethany House Publishers
11300 Hampshire Ave. S.
Minneapolis, MN 55438